# 'I don't want you to go either—'

Mark interjected, 'I'm not talking about friendship, Ginny, I'm talking about sex.' His mouth tightened. 'Or, more appropriately in this case, *lack* of sex.'

She recoiled. 'But th-that's absurd,' she stammered, shaking her head wildly. 'Surely you don't believe that?'

He didn't move. 'There's one very easy way to find out.'

A New Zealand doctor with restless feet, **Helen Shelton** has lived and worked in Britain and travelled extensively. Married to an Australian she met while on safari in Africa, she recently moved to Sydney where they plan to settle for a little while at least. She has always been an enthusiastic reader and writer and inspiration for the background for her medical romances comes directly from her own experiences working in hospitals in several countries around the world.

**Recent titles by the same author:**

ONE MAGICAL KISS
CONTRACT DAD

# AN UNGUARDED MOMENT

## BY
## HELEN SHELTON

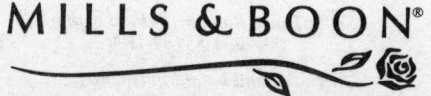

MILLS & BOON®

*All the characters in this book have no existence outside the imagination of the author, and have no relation whatsoever to anyone bearing the same name or names. They are not even distantly inspired by any individual known or unknown to the author, and all the incidents are pure invention.*

*All Rights Reserved including the right of reproduction in whole or in part in any form. This edition is published by arrangement with Harlequin Enterprises II B.V. The text of this publication or any part thereof may not be reproduced or transmitted in any form or by any means, electronic or mechanical, including photocopying, recording, storage in an information retrieval system, or otherwise, without the written permission of the publisher.*

*This book is sold subject to the condition that it shall not, by way of trade or otherwise, be lent, resold, hired out or otherwise circulated without the prior consent of the publisher in any form of binding or cover other than that in which it is published and without a similar condition including this condition being imposed on the subsequent purchaser.*

*MILLS & BOON and MILLS & BOON with the Rose Device are registered trademarks of the publisher.*

*First published in Great Britain 1999*
*Harlequin Mills & Boon Limited,*
*Eton House, 18-24 Paradise Road, Richmond, Surrey TW9 1SR*

© Poppytech Services Pty Ltd 1999

ISBN 0 263 81524 2

*Set in Times Roman 10 on 11½ pt.*
*03-9904-53144-D*

*Printed and bound in Norway*
*by AIT Trondheim AS, Trondheim*

# CHAPTER ONE

GINNY REID gritted her teeth.

Her knuckles where she gripped the telephone receiver had turned white, she saw, and she deliberately loosened her grasp, not wanting her frustration to become obvious to the anxious woman who sat opposite her. The last thing poor Mrs Atkins needed now was to see how difficult it was proving to get help for her ill son. If she was to continue to care for Warren what she needed was reassurance that effective back-up would always be available when she needed help.

'Doctor, this *is* urgent,' Ginny insisted again. 'My patient needs to be in hospital immediately.'

'Dr Reid, it simply isn't that straightforward,' the psychiatrist countered once more. 'I agree that Warren has chronic schizophrenia but nothing you've found, examining him today, suggests he's acutely psychotic. We've only one acute psychiatric bed left and that has to be kept for emergencies—'

'This *is* an emergency. He's taken no medication for a week.' Ginny raised her eyebrows at Mrs Atkins who nodded frantic, bird-like confirmation. 'His mother found the tablets under his bed and, remember, he refused his last two depot injections.'

'But he's orientated and co-operative.'

'He's withdrawn and preoccupied.'

'He's working.'

'He was fired two weeks ago.'

'The nurse who saw him yesterday—'

'Has only met him once before,' she grated, wishing

5

she'd thought to ask Mrs Atkins to wait outside through this. 'His usual psychiatric nurse is on maternity leave and the person covering him is so overworked that she can't get back for a fortnight. Warren's an extremely intelligent young man and he's good at covering but I've been his GP for five years and I know him well. I'm convinced he's relapsed and…and I don't think his family can cope with going through this again at home.' Or you'll have more than one patient on your hands, she added mentally, noting the panicky way Warren's mother had started to wring her hands. 'We must act quickly.'

'I'm not convinced there are sufficient grounds for admission right now.' The psychiatrist sounded harassed. 'Resources are—'

'Tight. Yes, I know.' She felt like screaming but still she struggled to keep the impatience out of her tone. She couldn't help but be aware of how badly health service changes had affected psychiatric services within the NHS; despite the staff's dedication and hard work the deficiencies were appallingly obvious every time she tried to organise an admission. 'But early intervention will be cost effective here. A brief period of assessment and therapy could stabilise Warren now and prevent a prolonged admission in a few weeks.'

There was a short pause then the other doctor said wearily, 'I can't agree to admit him directly now but I'll make space to see him myself in clinic tomorrow morning.'

Ginny let her breath out. She held up hopeful crossed fingers to Mrs Atkins. 'I'd appreciate that.'

'I'm not guaranteeing anything,' the psychiatrist warned.

But Ginny was confident of her assessment that Warren needed acute care and although the doctor was a new appointment to the local hospital she already had a reputation for being conscientious and thorough. Warren would be in good hands. 'Thank you for seeing him.'

'Ten-thirty.'

'Ten-thirty,' Ginny repeated, making a note on her jotter. 'So I'll call you…around twelve?'

'I'll call you,' the other woman said quickly, obviously not keen to have Ginny pursuing her through the department by telephone again.

Ginny repeated her thanks then replaced the receiver and turned towards Warren's mother with a relieved smile. 'Tomorrow morning at the hospital,' she told her. 'She'll do a full assessment.'

'Oh, thank you, Doctor.' With a lace handkerchief clutched in a shaking hand, Mrs Atkins dabbed at her eyes. 'I knew I could trust you to do something. I was so worried when the nurse told me he didn't need to see anyone. I know he's hearing the voices and he won't listen to me and with him not taking his medicine…' She lifted one frail arm helplessly. 'You're right, I couldn't go through…not like last time, not when the voices got so bad.'

'Hopefully we'll be able to control that this time,' Ginny said gently.

'And, Doctor, you know he's not eating. He won't say anything but I know he thinks we're trying to poison him— like he thought last time.'

'I remember.' Ginny knew how painful it had been for Mrs Atkins to discover that Warren had thought she was trying to harm him. She had never seemed an especially strong person but over the past five or so years since Warren's schizophrenia had been diagnosed Ginny had been moved by the dedication with which she cared for her son, care which hadn't flinched despite the end of her marriage.

Warren's father and her husband of more than thirty years had left the family soon after Warren's first breakdown and although Ginny had tried frantically to help him come to terms with his son's illness, including driving for several hours to see him at his brother's home in London where he'd been staying, he'd made it clear he wouldn't be back.

She showed Mrs Atkins out of her office. 'I'll come around if you're worried about anything or if Warren decides he's not keen to go up to the hospital. Just ring me.'

'Thank you, Doctor. You're very kind.' Mrs Atkins's smile looked marginally stronger.

Alone again, Ginny tipped herself back in her chair, lifted her feet to rest them on her desk and closed her eyes. Her temples had started to ache while she'd been speaking on the telephone and now she rubbed at them with her fingers. It had been a long day but thankfully Mrs Atkins had been her last appointment of the afternoon.

Her door opened and she looked up, smiling her thanks when the other GP in the small practice handed her a steaming cup of coffee.

'I thought you probably needed it,' Mark said. 'I could hear the argument you were having from next door. Long day?'

'Terrible day.' She took several long swallows of her drink and sighed her appreciation when he came up behind her and his warmly experienced fingers probed her shoulders through the cloth of her shirt, effortlessly finding the aching knots in the muscles beneath. 'Mmm, that's lovely, thanks. Wonderful. Exactly what I need. Naomi Dennison's breast biopsy showed tumour, Ray Kennings looks like he's going to lose that leg and you're right about me arguing— I was on the phone for more than twenty minutes, trying to persuade a psychiatrist to agree to assess Warren Atkins.'

She let him tilt her head back slightly, her eyes half closing as he massaged her temples. 'Why do I do this job?'

'Because you love it.' He sounded amused. 'And you love your patients, and if everything was straightforward and easy you'd be bored out of your mind.'

'But it doesn't have to be so difficult every day, all the time.' Mark's fingers were like magic—she'd never met anyone who could cure her headaches like him. 'Honestly, Mark, Warren's very unwell, yet it's been almost impossible to get expert help with him.'

His fingers circled gently, easing her aching forehead. 'You didn't pull strings, then?'

She flushed, not willing to admit that if Dr Thomas hadn't agreed to see Warren she'd have considered it.

'I'd have thought that being on intimate terms with the hospital's senior psychiatrist would earn you a few favours,' he continued dryly.

'I'm not sleeping with him,' Ginny snapped, her eyes opening sharply.

'Did I say that?'

But his gaze was unrepentant and mocking, and Ginny scowled. 'You implied it,' she grumbled. 'I've told you before, we're just friends. Don't stop—it's glorious.'

'I'm not stopping, I'm moving.' His fingers returned to the base of her neck. 'Lean forward. You're too stiff.'

'Stress.' Obediently she tipped her head forward. 'Not all men share your views on the most important reason for pursuing a relationship,' she told him. 'Neil's priority has never been sex.' Mark's laugh was irritating but, mellowed now by his massage, she elected to ignore it.

'Sarah might have changed you but I used to feel sorry for the women you dated. Heaven knows why most of them still think you're wonderful. To me it seemed as if the minute that first passion cooled, and you were able to keep your hands off them, that was it—they were out.'

'I've kept my hands off you,' he said softly. 'And we're still together.'

'Platonically and professionally. In the romantic sense of the word we've never dated,' she reminded him triumphantly. 'Which proves my point precisely. The only time you asked me out properly I turned you down.'

'When?'

'I can't believe you've forgotten.' Smiling, she jiggled her shoulders when his fingers stilled. 'Don't stop now. The pain's almost gone. You asked me to that student thing that time. The dress-up night where everyone was supposed to go as his or her favourite movie star.'

He laughed. 'That has to be far more than a decade ago and I only asked you because I felt sorry for you. It wasn't long after we first met and you had flu and your nose was bright red.'

'Still, you did ask me.' She sniffed. 'I turned you down because I felt too sick and you never asked me again.'

Lifting her head, she saw that his gaze had sharpened half-thoughtfully at that, and she laughed to show that her mock self-pity was merely a joke. 'Don't fret,' she teased, squeezing the warm hand on her shoulder. 'After all these years you're still safe with me.'

They'd been friends and partners for a total of almost fifteen years now, and although she understood why Mark was often pursued—as a woman she couldn't help but be aware of his attractiveness—their own friendship, despite being very close, had never been anything but platonic.

They'd never discussed the issue but she knew that it was an arrangement which suited each of them perfectly—herself, because he was the best friend she'd ever had and she'd never wanted to do anything that might risk that, and him because, she suspected, the ready availability of beautiful women and his inability until recently to commit to a long-term involvement with any of them meant he doubly valued their steady friendship and the stability of their business relationship.

'Your point about Neil is interesting, though, ethically,' she remarked, referring to his assumption she'd have used her friendship with the senior psychiatrist to speed up treatment for Warren. 'Do you refer your elderly patients directly to Sarah?'

His fingers had begun to move again but now, at the mention of the geriatric consultant he'd been seeing, they stilled once more and she realised that her question had ruffled him. 'Sometimes,' he admitted testily, reinforcing her suspicion. 'Not recently.'

'Oh?' Sarah was a dedicated geriatrician with a superb reputation so was she too overburdened to take on more patients? Or was, perhaps, the relationship between Mark and Sarah not what it had been? Ginny tilted her head back and eyed him. He'd seemed a little edgy lately. Perhaps this explained why. 'Has something happened recently?'

'This and that.' The brown gaze that met her wide green one was deliberately bland, but he stepped away from her abruptly and Ginny straightened, her curiosity prickled. Whenever she'd seen Mark and Sarah together they'd seemed very content, and she'd wondered if for the first time he might be contemplating a permanent relationship with someone.

In all honesty, Ginny admitted, the idea had left her feeling a little forlorn.

Now thirty-three, she'd never fallen in any more than 'like' with a man, and since she wasn't prepared to compromise on emotional involvement she was in the process of growing resigned to the idea that she might never marry. While the thought of remaining single didn't frighten her, the 'fulfilled, no-nonsense career-woman' façade she cultivated was not quite as thick as she'd have liked. In fact, until Sarah, the steady parade of women through Mark's life had left her hopeful that she might at least have some congenial company in her old age.

Of course, that thought was profoundly selfish, she acknowledged, disliking herself. She wanted him to be happy.

Besides, she told herself firmly, they'd been too close too long for marriage to Sarah to change much. 'Mark...?' she ventured hesitantly. 'I'm sorry if things aren't working out—'

He cut her off. 'That's enough, Gin.' His expression was guarded enough for her to know she wouldn't get anything more out of him. 'Ready to leave?'

She blinked, then realised what he meant and groaned. 'Oh, no, I forgot. First Tuesday of the month?'

'"GP management of heart failure",' he confirmed, quoting the evening's lecture topic as he opened her door. 'If we don't leave now we'll miss the start.'

'Heaven forbid,' she murmured, rummaging in a drawer for her bleeper. She wasn't on call but a couple of her most needy patients had her direct pager number. 'I suppose it beats another late night paperwork session.' She gulped the rest of her coffee then slid her arms into the dark woollen coat he'd retrieved from the back of the door. 'Mark, you're an angel, my headache's practically gone. What would I do without you?'

Instead of a teasing acknowledgement that he was, indeed, indispensable—the sort of comment that remark normally engendered—Mark's face tightened. 'You'd survive,' he said quietly, turning away so abruptly she knew he'd missed the sharp look she'd sent him.

Neither of them said much on the drive to the main hospital in Norwich, their nearest general hospital and around thirty minutes' journey in light traffic from their surgery in the pretty Norfolk village. Mark's replies to her questions about his day were monosyllabic and by the time they arrived Ginny was feeling distinctly unsettled. Never a moody person, it wasn't like Mark not to be good-humoured. If her questions about Sarah had irritated him, why hadn't he simply told her to mind her own business?

They went directly to the foyer where the GPs traditionally gathered before the lecture and joined a group of doctors near the door, collecting a juice each before the drug company representative hosting the meeting called them in for the start of the talk.

Despite her lack of enthusiasm tonight, these monthly meetings were usually interesting and informative but, conscious of Mark silent beside her and disturbed by his quietness, Ginny found it difficult to concentrate on the discussion on heart failure. Determined to pay attention, she leaned forward in her seat, holding her back straight, her hands clasped on the bench in front of her.

At the end of the talk there was a sprinkling of questions from the audience then a brief burst of applause before the doctors began to file towards the door. The visiting consultant who'd given the talk had prepared a summary for them to take away and she accepted his notes with a murmur of thanks as she left the theatre.

As was normal after these meetings the company sponsoring the talk had arranged dinner for all the doctors, and Ginny automatically followed the others towards the buffet. While Mark was waylaid by another of their colleagues, wanting to know about some golf game the following week, Ginny dished a few things onto a plate. She selected a quiet corner and picked at a few morsels of green salad, managing to summon a thin smile for the grey-haired senior partner from another local practice when he approached.

'There you are, Virginia.' Donald's tone suggested she'd been hiding somewhere. He inspected her food and clicked his tongue disapprovingly. 'Good Lord, woman! You've the figure of a twenty-year-old. Don't tell me you've taken up this dieting fad?'

'I had a good lunch,' she said, deliberately keeping her voice light as she wondered what he'd have said if she'd been overweight. Probably that she shouldn't have dressing on her salad, she acknowledged wearily, reminding herself for what felt like the hundredth time that he was of a generation when remarks such as that were not considered impolite.

Donald's partnership and her own shared the area's night and weekend on-call rota and practice manager, helping enormously to reduce practice expenses and improve the after-hours service for their patients, so although Donald's sexist manner often grated she did her best to ignore it. Mark tended to be less tolerant, but Donald was a good, experienced GP and for the sake of peace and a workable roster he, too, made an effort to keep relations sweet.

'How's Mary?' she asked.

Donald beamed. 'Very well. She's been home two weeks now. I wanted to thank you for all your help. The obstetrician was very complimentary about your antenatal care.'

Ginny's smile eased into a more genuine one. Her role in the practice included covering obstetrics and she'd recently supervised his daughter's pregnancy. 'She was a model patient.'

'Ha! You're being too modest. That daughter of mine's never been a model anything. You handled her perfectly. I only hope that new baby of hers gives her less trouble than she gave us as a youngster.' Donald laughed grimly. 'She just about drove her poor mother mad!'

'I'm sure no offspring of yours would behave in any way other than perfectly,' Ginny said diplomatically.

Mark joined them, laden plate in hand, his brows lifting at Donald's shout of laughter. 'Who's not behaving perfectly?'

Ginny wrinkled her nose at him when she saw the pointed look he directed at the hand Donald had rested casually on her waist as they'd spoken. Despite Donald's age, Mark was convinced he had designs on her. 'He's after you,' he'd warned, after he'd caught Donald giving her a sloppily drunken kiss at their last Christmas party. 'Watch out.'

At the time Ginny had laughed for while she'd found the brief embrace unpleasant she'd been confident the only reason for it had been harmless high spirits, in both senses of the word. Subsequently, though, she'd sensed a certain wary watchfulness in Mark when it came to Donald, as if the elder doctor's actions had put Mark's protective instincts on full alert.

'I was congratulating your lovely partner on her management of Mary's pregnancy.' Donald greeted Mark with a nod, promptly removed his hand from Ginny and picked up a slice of buttered baguette, waving it in the air as he spoke. 'She was the only GP in the district brave enough to take her on—the others were all too frightened of me!'

'Oh, Ginny loves a challenge,' Mark answered. He lifted a forkful of potato salad, his eyes meeting hers briefly and knowingly. 'She likes something to get her teeth into.'

'And my daughter would have been tough.' Donald laughed again. 'When her mother was alive she was just the same. Brain full of cotton wool.'

'That's absurd,' Ginny argued, her smile stiff as she confronted him. 'Mary only wanted what was best for her baby.'

'Well, I for one am pleased my first grandson wasn't born in a swimming pool full of dolphins,' announced Donald. 'That was her plan before I sent her along to talk to you.' He sighed. 'I don't understand the strange ideas people come up with these days, and I've given up trying to argue with my crazy daughter.'

She gave him a reproving look. 'Mary's one of the least crazy people I've met. All she and Giles needed was a little information and gentle guidance. She'll be a wonderful mother.'

'Hmm.' He sounded unconvinced. 'She's given up asking me for medical advice. I hope she doesn't start pestering you.'

'I'll look forward to seeing her,' Ginny said. 'Following up pregnancies I've been involved with is one of my favourite parts of the job.'

'Any plans for babies yourself, then?'

Ginny blinked. 'That's hardly relevant,' she responded stiffly, exchanging a pained look with Mark.

Apart from an exasperated roll of his eyes, he didn't come to her rescue and Donald was chuckling, peering at her over his glasses. 'The rumour goes that you've been seeing that psychiatrist chap for a while now, haven't you? Seems a nice enough fellow.'

'Neil is a good friend,' she said edgily. 'But I'm a career woman, Donald.'

'That's what they all say at first,' he countered. 'Sounds to me like you haven't found the right man to get your baby hormones flowing.'

'Perhaps I never will,' she said briskly, blinking quickly, determined not to let him think his comment might have bothered her. 'When are you going to realise that not every woman is destined for a life of domesticity and nappies?'

Mark's sharpened gaze suggested she perhaps hadn't shielded her sensitivity about the issue well enough but Donald, apparently oblivious, continued unmuted. 'Just you wait,' he announced, nudging Mark, whom Ginny could sense growing increasingly irritated beside her. 'I give her six months,' he continued. 'If that psychiatrist doesn't pull his socks up someone else will sweep her off her feet. I'll be tempted myself! Ha! Ha!'

'I wouldn't bother,' Mark muttered tightly. 'You'd have to be twenty years younger before she'd even look twice—'

'That's enough!' Ginny directed her glare towards her partner. 'You're talking nonsense, the pair of you.' We do not need any arguments, she said silently with her eyes, appreciating his attempt to shield her from Donald's banter but not wanting to upset the older man. Leave it. I can handle him.

Donald was still laughing, apparently oblivious both to her tension and to the animosity she could feel radiating from Mark. 'You might be surprised,' Donald told Mark. 'I've had a reputation as quite a ladies' man in the past.'

'A reputation I can quite understand.' Sending her partner another warning look, Ginny smiled appeasingly. She swallowed her own exasperation by reminding herself yet again how difficult it had been to co-ordinate cover with a locum service. It had taken more than a year to persuade Donald and his partner, both old-fashioned GPs used to endless hours on call, to join them in covering the area's after-hours work.

Falling out with Donald and jeopardising the arrangement would be worse than unfortunate. For when Donald's partnership was on call their patients received far better after-hours care than if Ginny and Mark had to rely on a service which provided temporary doctors unfamiliar with the area.

She and Mark had discussed this many times, and although Mark's throat moved convulsively when he eventually spoke it was evenly. 'Donald, I've been meaning to ask how the arrangements for the tournament are going.'

The elder man took the words at face value, obviously still blithely oblivious to the barely suppressed anger in Mark's voice, and was immediately diverted into a discussion on the golfing skills of their fellow local GPs and the difficulties in assembling them in one place on one particular day.

After a few minutes Ginny muttered an excuse and left the two men. She didn't share Mark's enthusiasm for sport and it seemed as good an opportunity as any to escape.

She dodged from cluster to cluster of doctors, a smile

fixed to her face, making small talk. Later, she joined a group of three other doctors at the pharmaceutical display, letting the rep's slick patter slide over her head as she puzzled over Mark's behaviour. Donald was frequently irritating but Mark was normally better at concealing his reaction.

She bit at her lower lip and glanced towards where he stood near the lecture theatre entrance, talking with another GP. He was still speaking but, as if he'd sensed her regard, he glanced up and their eyes met. Instead of acknowledging her, he simply returned her stare broodingly before he looked away.

Something was definitely wrong. It couldn't just be that he was annoyed with her for questioning him about Sarah—Mark wasn't so sensitive—so it had to be something else. Was it work? Then why had he looked at her as if he were seeing someone he hardly knew?

Ginny held her breath then deliberately swivelled back towards the rep, focusing on his thin, pale face and struggling to keep her attention on his speech—a little spiel about the usefulness of his company's product following a coronary.

'Repeated studies have shown it reduces left ventricular enlargement and thus subsequent development of heart failure,' he was saying earnestly. 'Even in the absence of documented hypertension.'

She shook her head slowly. The data were indisputable and she used a similar product for that same reason—that it reduced the risk of heart failure after a heart attack—but, however much she hated the restraints herself, the salesman clearly wasn't in touch with current realities in general practice. 'But isn't it considerably more expensive than rival drugs?'

He sniffed. 'We believe our product is vastly superior,' he said aloofly, giving her a patronising look.

'In what way?'

He frowned. 'Improved packaging, better formulation, improved patient compliance,' he said, reeling off the words he'd clearly learned by heart. 'Plus many other features too numerous to list.' He picked up a sheaf of papers and waved them in front of her face. 'All discussed in the literature. I can give you copies, Dr Reid.'

But tonight she wasn't in the mood to be fobbed off like that. Aware of the amused glances of her colleagues, she waved the papers away. 'These are superficial changes,' she said bluntly. 'How do you justify trebling the price?'

He blanched. 'Uh…we have an enormous research budget to support,' he muttered vaguely.

'An enormous bribery budget, you mean,' she said irritably. 'Twice in the last month your company has offered me free holidays abroad in return for agreeing to prescribe your products. Is that ethical advertising?'

'Th-they were invitations to conferences,' he stammered. 'Not holidays.'

'My reading of the brochures suggested they were offering two hours of speeches and two weeks of sunbathing.'

His gaping mouth stopped her tirade before it had really started. With a guilty start she realised she was taking out her stressful day and her foreboding about Mark on this man who, after all, was only doing his job. 'I'm sorry,' she said in a brittle voice, managing a thin smile. 'Your company has several good products but it annoys me to see so much money wasted in promoting them.'

'Plenty of GPs find our conferences educational,' he said defensively. 'We had over a hundred at our last one in Malaga.'

'So I believe,' she said dryly, mentally trying to calculate what the trips to Spain must have added to the NHS drugs bill. The answer was too horrific to contemplate. 'Excuse me, please.' She shook her head at the rep's rather lame offer of a complimentary pocket torch.

She turned away to find Mark there. 'Even for you, that was a bit over the top,' he said quietly.

She met his dark gaze unflinchingly. 'Let's just say I'm not at my most cheerful tonight.'

Mark dumped his glass on a table behind the pharmaceutical display and took her elbow. 'If it's any consolation, I've had a hell of a day too,' he rasped. 'Let's get out of here. We have to talk.'

'Well, hooray for that,' Ginny muttered heartily, skipping to keep up as he steered her towards the glass doors which opened towards the car park. 'Get it off your chest, whatever it is.'

He ignored that. 'Quickly, Ginny. Donald's right behind us.' He pushed open the doors and hurried her into the breezy chill of the April night. 'If I have to see him pawing you again I swear I'll take a swing at him.'

'He wasn't *pawing* me.' She gave him an exasperated look but didn't dally, wanting another encounter with Donald as little as he did. 'And if you ever take a swing at him, I'll take one at you. What on earth's wrong with you tonight?'

'Call it a crisis of conscience,' he muttered cryptically, swinging her towards where his black Audi gleamed darkly under the orange glow of a streetlight. 'Better still—a turning-point.'

Ginny eyed him warily. 'I have no idea what you're talking about.'

'Do you want the good news or the bad?' He pointed his keys at the car and the lights blinked a welcome. 'Get in.'

When he next spoke they were several miles from the hospital and almost at the edge of town. 'Donald was right about Neil,' he said quietly, almost idly she'd have said except that she knew Mark never said or did anything idly. 'You have been seeing him a long time.'

She sent him a sharp look and he clicked his tongue. 'All right, you're just friends,' he added. 'Still…'

'Donald was talking rubbish as usual.' She watched the trees blur as he accelerated onto the dual carriageway. 'He can't accept that all women aren't pre-programmed for motherhood.'

Mark's hands shifted on the steering-wheel. 'He's just thinking about impregnating you himself,' he said, his voice roughening. 'Probably spends most nights fantasising about it.'

'Don't be ridiculous.' Ginny rolled her eyes. 'All this is in your head. He's old!'

'Not that old. He's been widowed five years and he's sizing up his chances.' His mouth tightened. 'He's so obvious he makes me sick.'

'I could do worse,' she taunted. 'He's rich.'

'Horrible woman.' But he grinned, a lazy, wry grin that dissolved the flare of tension between them. 'Donald gets to you the same as he does me. Stop trying to provoke me.' He indicated and turned off the carriageway onto the road that led to their village. 'You're particularly scratchy tonight, aren't you?'

'No more than you.'

His face flashed briefly orange at a corner light and she saw his smile stiffen. 'I told you, it's been a hard day,' she said quickly. 'I'm tired and I'm ratty and since something's obviously bothering you as well why don't you just tell me what it is I've done wrong and let us both relax?'

'You haven't done anything.' But she saw his mouth had tightened again and the brief glance he sent her was unreadable. 'That poor drug rep tonight didn't know what hit him.'

'You know you agree with me about that,' she argued.

'That doesn't mean I think it's fair to squabble with the man. He doesn't make company policy.'

'I'm aware of that,' she said testily, 'but there's no harm in letting him know how we feel. Maybe they'll stop trying to bombard us with bribes.'

'Unlikely.'

'I know, I know.' Ginny leaned her aching head against the seat rest and sighed, resigning herself to the fact that he wouldn't tell her anything until it suited him. 'Let's just say I made a gesture.'

'An empty one.' He slowed for a traffic roundabout then drove through it and turned into the shrub-lined driveway that led up to his beautifully restored Tudor home, driving past her car to park in the dark-beamed garage which had once been a barn. 'You'll come in for coffee?'

It was more of a statement than a question and Ginny nodded automatically. They normally had coffee together after an evening out, and tonight especially she wanted to hear what he had to say.

While he prepared drinks she sat on one of the stools she'd bought him for his birthday three or four years earlier. 'You need a barber,' she mused, studying the way his dark, thick hair brushed the top of his collar.

He grinned suddenly. 'Stay away, Gin,' he warned. 'Last time I let you cut it I spent two weeks reassuring people I wasn't an escaped prisoner.'

Ginny smiled at the memory. He had looked rather alarming. Tall and athletically built, Mark was good-looking enough to turn most women's heads but he needed to wear his hair longer than a crew cut to soften his appearance. 'That was years ago,' she chided. 'We were poverty-stricken students—and I wasn't offering to cut it myself, just pointing out that if you haven't had time to make an appointment you must be working too hard.'

'We're both working too hard,' he said easily. Despite

his size he was never clumsy and he moved with easy efficiency around the room, each action spare and controlled as he organised the coffee. 'That's the nature of the job.'

He'd taken off his suit jacket and slung it across one of the other stools. While he waited for the water to boil he rolled up his shirtsleeves impatiently, the very masculine gesture revealing strong hair-roughened forearms. 'I like what you've done with *your* hair. It suits you like that.'

Ginny lifted a self-conscious hand to smooth her three-day-old bob. Her hair was dark with a slight wave and she normally wore it shoulder length and tied back, but she'd had it cut short to brush her chin this week, thinking the style would be cooler for summer. 'I thought you hadn't noticed.'

'Of course I noticed.'

'You didn't say anything.'

'I meant to.'

He'd had other things on his mind—Sarah perhaps, she realised, aware of a faintly piqued tinge of resentment at the thought. Abruptly she felt foolish. Of course it hadn't mattered that he hadn't said anything about her haircut. Until that moment she hadn't even realised she cared, and it was a ridiculously childish thing to have worried about. 'D-did you manage to fit in your squash game today?'

He nodded, looking down as he held the lid of the coffee-grinder. 'At lunchtime,' he replied loudly over the noise of the beans, being crushed. 'My calls finished late. I spent a long time this afternoon with Nellie Jarvis.'

'How is she?'

He frowned as he tipped the ground coffee into the plunger and filled it with the boiling water. 'Not well but she still refuses to go into hospital. I'm worried that we won't be able to keep her pain under control at home. She really should start on the opiates now but she refuses one of them. She hates the way it muddles her head.'

'What about the hospice?'

'We've discussed it but she's determined to stay at home.'

'And her daughters?' She followed him through into the living area.

'They're worried about her being in pain but they don't want to force her to leave.'

She settled herself at the opposite end of the sofa, accepting her drink with a murmur of thanks. 'They sound very sensible.'

'They are.' He sipped his coffee. 'I've asked one of the Macmillan nurses to pop round and see them. Hopefully she'll be able to give some advice about altering Nellie's analgesia to make it acceptable to her. She doesn't need to suffer and it'll be much easier for her daughters to cope if they know she's pain-free.'

Ginny nodded. Death and dying were issues that they each dealt with regularly, and her experiences in hospitals had strengthened her belief that terminally ill people such as Nellie should be encouraged to stay at home if that was what they wanted.

She took a mouthful of hot coffee then leaned back against the couch and closed her eyes with a sigh. 'This room is so peaceful.'

She heard him lower his cup and move and minutes later he was back, holding out two white tablets. 'I guess my massage wasn't enough, hmm? Paracetamol.'

'Exactly what I need.' Ginny nodded her thanks then took the pills and swallowed them with some of her coffee. 'And your massage was wonderful, as always.'

'You get too many headaches.'

'Stress.'

'Listen to some relaxation tapes.'

She groaned. 'Just take half my workload away.'

'I wish I could.' Mark didn't even smile. Instead, he

strode restlessly to a cabinet on the other side of the room and poured himself a generous whisky. He regarded her over the rim. 'Ginny, there's something we have to discuss,' he said heavily.

'You're leaving me,' Ginny said lightly, joking to overcome a sudden jolt of nervousness brought on by his seriousness. 'You're quitting.'

Mark stilled, his expression immediately guarded, and she paled. 'Tell me I'm wrong,' she said hollowly. 'You're not really quitting, are you?'

# CHAPTER TWO

'SARAH'S been offered a consultant post in Aberdeen.'

So Ginny herself hadn't done anything wrong—this was all about Sarah. Despite her concern for how the break-up of Mark's relationship might affect him, Ginny felt herself relax. For a few seconds he'd really had her worried that he was actually resigning. 'She's going to take it?'

'Yes.'

Although Ginny knew Sarah was originally from Scotland, she'd seemed settled in Norwich and, beyond that, very fond of Mark. 'I thought she was happy at the Norfolk?'

'It's only a locum,' he told her. 'The funding isn't approved to make it a permanent appointment, and may never be. Aberdeen offers her a secure position in an established service and she'll be close to her family. She's very enthusiastic.'

No wonder Mark was unhappy. Aberdeen was so far away that it'd be enormously difficult to maintain a relationship. Gently she asked, 'Does this mean goodbye for you both?'

'Not necessarily.'

'You're still trying to persuade her to stay?'

'She's asked me to go with her.'

'Oh.' Ginny felt suddenly very cold. She looked down at her coffee then carefully placed the cup on the table lest her shaking hands dropped it. 'Oh.' She studied the carpet. 'Oh.' Realising she sounded like an idiot, she stammered, 'Wh-when? When are you leaving?'

'I didn't say I was, definitely.'

Her eyes flew to his shadowed face. 'You said—'

'That Sarah wanted me to.' He was brusque now. 'I didn't say I'd made up my mind.'

Ginny wondered about that. 'But, of course, you're considering it?'

'Yes.' He lifted one broad shoulder. 'It's only fair to let you know what's going on. I want you to understand that I wouldn't leave you in the lurch. If I do end up in Scotland—and it is still an ''if''—it wouldn't be until I'd found someone suitable to buy my share of the practice.'

'Thank you.' She stared at him dully. 'Well...I don't know what to say.' She blinked. 'I'll miss you.'

They exchanged faint smiles and Mark said, 'Me too.'

'W-will you marry?'

He shrugged dismissively as if the idea wasn't particularly important. 'I'm still trying to decide between Scotland and Norfolk.'

'Surely the decision's between Sarah and Norfolk?'

'Whatever.' Mark took another mouthful of his drink.

'When...if you go to Aberdeen,' she said hesitantly, 'what will you do there? Join a practice? Locum?'

'There's a rumoured vacancy for a senior lecturer in general practice. Sarah's spoken to the department and they're interested in seeing my CV.'

So his plans really were more advanced than he'd implied. 'You've always said that you'd like to teach eventually,' she answered, realising she sounded stilted and formal. 'I thought you meant taking on a trainee at the practice.' She blinked quickly. 'But, of course, a lectureship would be much better.'

'Yes.'

'This sounds like the perfect opportunity.'

'Perhaps.'

'When?'

'Sarah's leaving in July.'

Three months. Ginny met his enigmatic gaze with a weak smile. 'And this…lectureship in general practice. When would that start?'

'October.'

Six months. That meant there was plenty of time for them to find a replacement partner, she told herself, wondering why she didn't find the thought remotely consoling. Probably because six months didn't seem very long when she considered the length of time she and Mark had been together.

She stood abruptly, brushing non-existent dust from her skirt with an unsteady hand, suddenly desperate to escape. 'Well,' she said, her voice breathy now, 'this is all a bit of a surprise. Not at all what I was expecting.'

'I'm sorry.'

'There's nothing to be sorry about.' She summoned another faint smile. 'I…I'm just startled, that's all.'

She collected her handbag from the floor behind the couch. 'It was bound to happen some day. I don't know why I haven't been expecting it.' She realised she was flushing. 'I thought…silly of me really, but I thought we'd always be working together.'

When he didn't say anything she lowered her head and pushed her stockinged feet back into the shoes she'd discarded earlier. She turned towards the door and Mark reached ahead of her to open it, his eyes worried as he surveyed her strained expression. 'You're tired,' he said quietly. 'Stay if you like.'

'I'm fine.' Mark's home was like Ginny's second home. He kept a room made up for her and she often stayed over after an evening out simply to avoid the bother of driving two miles back to her flat in the village, but tonight…tonight it didn't feel right.

'Don't tell me you've caught this awful flu, Ginny.'

Ginny forced a smile to her face the next morning as she

looked up from the correspondence on her desk to greet Lynn, one of their two practice nurses. 'Do I look that bad?'

The elder woman nodded. 'Like you haven't slept for a week,' she said frankly.

'I was restless last night,' she admitted.

'You're working too hard,' Lynn scolded. 'You both are. Mark looks just as tired as you—worse even, if that's possible. You should get some locums in and go away for a fortnight. It's years since either of you took a decent holiday.'

Ginny made what she hoped was a suitably noncommittal sound. Mark would be getting away soon enough but he was the one who should break the news to the rest of the staff. 'I'll get an early night tonight,' she said abruptly. 'Has Beryl Scott been in to see you yet this morning?'

Lynn nodded, taking the hint with good grace. 'She's next door. I'd like you to have a look at her today. I've taken the dressing down and cleaned the wound but it's not looking as good as it did on Monday.'

Ginny pushed her chair back and followed the nurse into the clinical room. Beryl was a fifty-year-old woman with long-standing insulin-requiring diabetes. She'd been discharged from the local hospital a month ago after having had two gangrenous toes amputated. Despite regular, skilled attention from Lynn, her foot was taking a long time to heal.

'Hmm.' Ginny lifted off the sterile guard and peered down at the inflamed wound, the edges of which were darker than she was happy with. 'Running a temperature?'

'I was hot last night,' Beryl admitted, 'but there hasn't been any pain.'

That didn't mean anything. Beryl's diabetes meant that the sensation in her feet was impaired. 'How have your sugars been?'

'A bit up the last few days, Doctor. Seventeen this morning so I gave myself a couple more units.'

'Very wise.' Ginny was happy for Beryl to alter her own medication—she was an intelligent woman and very capable of managing that aspect of her diabetes—but the fact that her blood sugar control was slipping was further evidence that infection was taking hold. 'I'm afraid you're going to need at least a course of intravenous antibiotics and complete rest to get over this.'

Beryl sighed. 'I thought that might be the case. I warned my Bill this morning. I said, "That young Dr Reid will take one look at this and send me straight up to town."'

Ginny rested her hand on her patient's thin shoulder. 'I'm sorry, but you're right.' She hesitated over the next bit but it was her responsibility to warn her patient. 'You know there's always a possibility you'll need more surgery?'

She nodded. 'They told me that last time.' She sniffed. 'But me and Bill will manage, Doctor. We'll be all right.'

Ginny reflected on that comment as she waited on the telephone to speak to the surgical registrar on call for that day at the local general hospital. Beryl was the sort of practical, cheerful person she should take a lesson from, she decided. There was no point in her working herself into a depression about Mark's news last night. Life had to go on. They'd remain friends, albeit at a distance, and perhaps finding a replacement for him wouldn't be the drawn-out trauma she was envisaging.

As usual, telephoning the hospital with a referral took at least fifteen minutes so she held the receiver to her ear with her shoulder while she took the opportunity to enter the details of Beryl's visit on the computer. Normally she waited until the end of a session to input information on all the patients she'd seen but at least this way she wasn't wasting her time while she waited on the phone.

As was standard, she was shunted through various wards and departments, finally being put through to Theatres where she was told that the registrar was scrubbed and operating and unable to come to the telephone.

After five years she should have been used to it but it was still intensely irritating. At least Beryl was the first patient of the day and she wasn't trying to organise her admission in the middle of a busy clinic. 'Put me back to the operator, please,' she requested wearily.

The theatre staff had had no idea how long it would be before the registrar was free to return her call, and if she sent Beryl directly to Casualty without a formal referral she might have to wait hours before being seen so she asked to be put through to the consultant who'd performed her original surgery, Bryan Gould.

'Bryan, it's Ginny Reid here.'

'Lovely to hear from you, Ginny.' The surgeon's greeting was warmly familiar. 'How's the squash?'

She grimaced. Mark and Bryan were great friends and they regularly played squash together. Bryan had organised a few games for her with his wife, Jane, but so far Ginny had managed to duck out of the arrangement. 'We haven't played yet,' she answered carefully.

He chuckled. 'Why aren't I surprised? Mark bet me fifty pounds I wouldn't get you onto the court. You're not going to make me lose my money, are you?'

'Quite probably,' she warned, making a mental note to rebuke Mark for taking Bryan's money like that. 'I actually wanted to talk to you about Beryl Scott. You remember her?'

'Of course. Has that wound healed yet?'

'It's getting worse. It's infected and I'm worried about how viable the next toe is. I think she should be admitted for antibiotics at least. I haven't had any luck getting through to the registrar on call. May I send her up?'

'Of course. Ask her to come directly to my clinic. I'll take a look myself.'

'Thanks. Maybe I'll organise that squash game after all.'

'Good girl!' She could hear a smile in his voice. 'You'll love it.'

Unlikely, she thought, replacing the receiver. She wrote a brief covering note and then took it through to where Beryl was waiting, her foot rebandaged and her crutches by her side. 'Mr Gould will see you in his clinic, and if he agrees it's necessary he'll arrange for you to be admitted. OK?'

Beryl nodded. 'Right you are, Doctor. Lynn is just arranging a cab for me. Ten minutes, she thinks.'

'Good.' Ginny smiled. 'Give the practice a call when you get out so we know when to come and see you.'

By the time she was settled back in her office there were half a dozen patients waiting to see her.

The village was small but they drew patients from about six miles around, meaning they had a moderately large practice with just under four thousand patients between Mark and herself. As it was primarily an ageing population, with younger people often leaving the area for Norwich, Yarmouth, or even London in search of employment, the workload was still high.

A large proportion of the younger patients who asked specifically to see her were women with gynaecological or obstetric queries. Ginny enjoyed this aspect of her work and was quite happy to carry the bulk of this load. The fact that all but two of her patients that morning were women was not unusual.

Mark took a special interest in paediatrics. At one stage he'd even toyed with the idea of a career in children's medicine but to Ginny's relief had instead decided to join her in general practice.

Now, although they were each trained in both fields, she

generally looked after the mothers while Mark took charge of their offspring. It was an arrangement which suited them both. All the other aspects of the job, the medical and surgical sides, as well as the administration they both hated, were evenly split.

By the time she'd finished her clinic Mark had already left for his house calls, and she ate lunch alone in the kitchen, flicking through the morning's delivery of pathology reports from the local laboratory while she munched her crisps.

Dr Thomas, the psychiatrist who'd agreed to see Warren Atkins, rang her soon after she sat down. 'I don't believe he's sectionable,' she said once she'd explained that she concurred with her opinion, 'but thankfully he's agreed to come in as a voluntary patient. I'll call you in a week or so and let you know how he's getting on.'

After making a note on her jotter to call in on Mrs Atkins the following day, Ginny looked up and smiled when Lynn breezed in with the computer printout of their list for the afternoon.

'Only eight for you and three for me,' she said happily. 'Barring any "urgents". Time to do a proper job.'

Ginny nodded, knowing what she meant. One of the most frustrating things she found about general practice was that the urge to do the job well was not always matched by the time in which to do it. When she took longer than scheduled with a patient she was always conscious that it was at the expense of keeping others waiting.

Happily this clinic was normally an exception, catering for 'well women' who'd not come to her with a specific problem but simply for a general screening check-up and discussion. It was the best opportunity she had in the week to practise preventative medicine. Years of failing to make an impact meant she was quite resigned to her lack of success in persuading the rest of her patients to give up smoking and switch to healthier diets, but in this clinic, at least, she was sure she did some good.

She checked Lynn's list, noting that six of the patients she'd be seeing needed routine cervical smears. The practice sent out reminders when these were due and the receptionist followed up women who didn't attend with a phone call to check that they'd either had their examination elsewhere or would make an appointment soon.

Her first patient was a mother of five from another village whom Ginny knew only vaguely because the only other time she'd been to see her was at her check-up when she'd joined the practice four years before. Unfortunately she was rather put out at what she called 'harassment' by the practice about attending for a smear.

'I'm sorry you feel like that.' Ginny tried to dampen her patient's annoyance with a firm but apologetic smile. 'But it's one of the few tests we have that directly detects the changes that occur before cancer develops and so treatment is straightforward. I know it can be uncomfortable—I dread them myself—but it only takes a few minutes.'

Mrs O'Reilly sniffed, looking vaguely mollified. 'Even you, being a doctor and all—you dread them?'

'Worse than the dentist,' Ginny admitted, and it was true. 'But I keep telling myself that two minutes of discomfort is worth it if it means any problem is caught early.'

Her patient clicked her tongue. 'I suppose that sounds fair. Lord knows what the family would do if I got sick.' She sat up on the bed and eyed the trolley doubtfully. 'Are you going to warm that thing up?'

Ginny smiled, knowing the battle was over. 'It's warm, I promise.'

A few minutes later Mrs O'Reilly sat up, her expression surprised. 'Well, who would have known it? I hardly felt a thing.'

'That's the way it should be.' Ginny fixed the slide, labelled it with a pencil, then removed her gloves and washed her hands. 'Do you examine your breasts regularly?'

Her patient grimaced. 'Not as a rule,' she admitted. 'I suppose I wouldn't mind learning how.'

Ginny waited for her to undress then studied the contours of her breasts. There was no obvious irregularity. 'The best time to check them is after your period. The breasts are naturally more lumpy before it. I find it best to do it in the bath or shower when my hands are soapy and they can glide over the skin. Check yourself in the mirror and then just feel around each part of the breast in turn, gently but firmly.'

She showed her patient how to move her fingers around each quadrant of the breast. 'That's exactly right. Finish off by checking under the arms. Good. That's it. A few minutes once a month.'

'And if I find something?' Mrs O'Reilly sat up, looking concerned. 'How will I know if it's important?'

'After a while you'll get to know your breasts well enough to know whether what you're feeling is new or not. If you do find a lump or anything at all that worries you it only takes a few minutes for me to check, and I'd much rather you came into the surgery than sit at home, worrying about it. The vast majority of lumps are cysts or simply prominent tissue and nothing to worry about.'

She left her patient to get dressed while she filled in the details on the specimen form then looked up with a smile when Mrs O'Reilly came back into the office. 'All right?'

'Thanks, Doctor, I feel much better now. I suppose I've just been putting it off because I was worried you might find something.'

In Ginny's experience, that, more than the fear of the discomfort, was by far the most common reason for women delaying their examination. 'Everything looked perfectly normal, Mrs O'Reilly. We'll drop you a note with your results when they come through.'

Lynn came in a few minutes later and collected the slides she needed for her own clinic. She grinned at Ginny. 'You did a good job with that one,' she said lightly. 'She's out there in the waiting-room, berating the rest of them for waiting too long between smears. "We all dread them," she's saying. "Dr Reid hates having them herself, but it only takes two minutes and it might save your life."'

'Amazing.' Ginny laughed. 'I've made an impression. Mrs O'Reilly's made my day.'

As she left, Lynn opened the door and called for Ginny's next patient. 'Cindy here might take longer,' she said quietly. 'Her John's being made redundant next month. I expect she needs a chat.'

Ginny nodded. Lynn's knowledge of the community was invaluable, particularly as she and Mark were both relative strangers to the village. Five years barely counted when many of the inhabitants had lived here for generations. Since in general practice there was often more behind a visit than the simple physical ailments complained of, there'd been many occasions when Lynn had been able to supply the missing link in an otherwise puzzling consultation.

The clinic went well, steadily, with no emergencies to interrupt, and by five-thirty Ginny had seen everyone and even brought her computer records up to date. Lynn told her that Mark was with his last patient and she gave him a few minutes to finish then peeked in. 'Need a coffee?'

'Desperately.' He summoned a grin for her but Ginny could sense his distraction and she saw tension in the weary way he eased himself away from his terminal. 'Finished already? That has to be a record.'

Ginny shrugged. 'Must be the warm weather.'

He joined her in the tiny kitchen at the rear of the surgery and over coffee Ginny steered the conversation towards work, still a little too unsettled by his news last night to talk about the future.

But when he was pouring them both a second drink Mark said, 'Sarah called me earlier to confirm dinner tomorrow. Had you remembered?'

Ginny hesitated. 'I don't mind if she cancels,' she said carefully. 'Aren't you...I mean, isn't she busy making plans?'

'She's not moving for another three months,' Mark said coolly. 'I think that gives her time enough to manage a small dinner party, don't you?'

Ginny promptly felt mean-spirited. Not dwelling on the reasons behind her reluctance to see Sarah right now she said hollowly, 'I suppose so.'

'You remember where her flat is?'

'She invited Neil as well and I'm going to ask him for a lift.' She'd only visited Sarah's home once, months ago, one night when Sarah had been on call and unexpectedly busy at the hospital and Mark had offered her Sarah's ticket to the theatre and they'd had to go there to collect both tickets. Ginny couldn't recall anything except that it had been in a modern, convoluted subdivision but Neil was good at finding places like that.

Lynn poked her head round the door and grinned at them. 'Jeff Morgan's managed to slice his arm open with a butcher's knife. Anyone interested?'

'I'll come,' Mark said immediately. 'I'm on call, anyway.' Instead of leaving directly, he stopped in the doorway, half in, half out. 'Get a decent night's sleep tonight, hmm?'

'Lynn's already told me I look haggard,' Ginny said tersely. 'Thanks, anyway.'

He laughed. 'You couldn't look *haggard* if you tried,'

he said easily, starting to pull the door shut, 'although you're good with grumpy and prickly.'

'Ha. Ha.' But he was already gone, and she slumped, letting her eyes close wearily. She *was* grumpy and prickly, she acknowledged, as well as stressed and uptight still about his news. She vowed to try harder to resign herself to him leaving.

Neil picked her up from her flat the next evening. 'I had lunch with our new psychiatrist, Myra Thomas, today,' he told her, *en route* to Sarah's flat. 'She called you a bull-dozer.'

Ginny laughed. 'Because I bulldozed her into admitting my patient?'

'Sounds as if it was appropriate,' he said lightly.

'What? My patient being admitted or her calling me a bulldozer?' Ginny teased.

'Both.' He smiled back.

'So you had lunch?' Ginny arched her brows at him. 'Interesting. I thought you were always too busy for lunch.'

'She's an excellent conversationalist.'

'Single?'

'Uh...divorced, I believe.'

She'd already noted the flush of colour at his cheeks so she wasn't fooled by his deliberate airiness.

Neil was a sweet, gentle person, and when they'd first met she'd wondered if he might be the sort of man she was looking for. After a few awkward embraces they'd realised there was no physical spark between them and they'd drifted into the casual and convenient friendship they now shared. Still, she knew him well enough to know he wanted romance in his life but, not wanting to embarrass him, she didn't ask anything else about the new psychiatrist. Mentally, though, she crossed her fingers for him, wishing she found it easier to wish Mark the same success with Sarah.

She was nervous about the evening. Mark had been edgy all day and she'd worked out that, after warning her of the possibility on Tuesday, tonight would be the perfect occasion to announce that he was definitely leaving and possibly even his engagement to Sarah.

She'd spent a few minutes already in front of the mirror, rehearsing a sort of stoical *bonhomie*, but she still wasn't confident she'd be able to carry it off with any sincerity. She told herself she just needed more time to get used to the idea, but still she was more than a little shocked by her selfishness.

There was a delay after Neil rang the bell outside Sarah's flat, and when Mark finally opened the door to them Ginny immediately registered his distracted smile and tousled hair. Her set smile froze. Had they interrupted Sarah's and Mark's...celebration?

Sarah promptly appeared, and confirmed the impression that they'd been making love for the attractive blonde's normally immaculately made-up face was bare and flushed, her dress slightly uneven, as if hastily fastened, and her smile definitely strained. 'Dinner's late,' she said huskily, kissing the air beside Ginny's cheek vaguely as she accepted the wine she'd brought, 'but come through.'

Ginny was embarrassed. She shot a quick look at Neil but his pleasant smile suggested he hadn't noticed anything amiss. Keeping her eyes averted, she handed Mark her coat and followed their hostess into the kitchen.

When Sarah opened the fridge to deposit their wine Ginny noted several bottles of chilling champagne, further confirmation of what she guessed was to come later in the evening. 'What a lovely flat,' she said stiffly, refraining from any mention of Sarah being about to leave it. 'And I love your garden. How on earth do you find time?'

'It's not easy.' Now they were unobserved Sarah's smile was suddenly little short of frigid, and Ginny caught her breath.

There were sounds behind her, suggesting that the two men had followed them, and Sarah's eyes promptly jerked away from Ginny to acknowledge Mark. 'Sweetheart, would you fix the drinks, please? I'll finish dinner.'

*Sweetheart*? Ginny looked quickly at Mark, surprised by the endearment. Mark was not the sort of man who suited being called something so...homely.

It seemed he disagreed for, apart from meeting Ginny's raised eyebrows with a brief, pointed frown that warned her to keep her mouth shut, he merely nodded. 'Ginny? Neil? Wine? Beer?'

Once they had drinks Sarah sent them into her living room, rejecting Ginny's hesitant offer of help with preparing the meal. Fortunately Neil was either oblivious to the atmosphere or chose to ignore it and he chatted easily with Mark, discussing golf and the deteriorating state of the health service with a relaxed calm that Ginny envied.

Mark was definitely unsettled. His responses, while polite, were clipped and his eyes shadowed as they studied Neil then flicked to her, and she realised that he was clearly as disturbed by their interruption as Sarah.

Her gaze was on his hands as he lifted them to make a point, and she wondered idly where they'd been making love. Here, downstairs, or in Sarah's bedroom?

Realising what she was thinking about, she started, shocked, but the images persisted. She already knew Mark was an inventive and passionate lover—too many of his ex-girlfriends had cried on her shoulder over the years for her not to have learned that—but that didn't mean she wanted to dwell on the fact. It felt like...an invasion of his privacy.

Abruptly she walked to the window and stared out into Sarah's beautifully tended garden. She leaned her heated forehead against the cool glass, disturbed by the direction her thoughts had taken.

Mark touched her shoulder, making her jump. 'All right?'

She turned hastily, surprised to see they were alone. 'Neil?'

'Talking to Sarah.'

Distantly, she could hear their voices. 'Gin, you're as stiff as a board,' he said, his hand drifting across to her other shoulder. 'Relax. You're supposed to be enjoying yourself. Drink your wine.'

She took a token sip and managed a small smile, but Mark knew her well enough to see through that. 'This is my fault, isn't it?' His arm slid to her elbow and he hugged her against him. 'I shouldn't have said anything about my leaving until—'

'Mark!' Whatever he'd been about to say was lost in Sarah's sharp exclamation as she appeared in the doorway, her eyes fixed on the arm that embraced Ginny. 'Dinner's almost ready,' she rasped. 'Choose some music.'

Not seeming to have noticed Sarah's annoyance, Mark simply withdrew his arm smoothly and swivelled to the CD player. He left Ginny confronting a tense Sarah whose eyes sparked with a fierce resentment Ginny didn't understand.

'Dinner smells good,' she ventured. 'Delicious.'

'Beef Wellington.' Sarah showed her teeth but it wasn't a smile.

'My favourite.'

Neil appeared behind Sarah, bearing a new bottle of wine. 'And mine. It looks fantastic.' Judging from his comments later, it tasted fantastic, too.

Although Ginny echoed Mark's and Neil's praise, Sarah's barely veiled hostility made her throat so tight that the bites of tender beef were as difficult to force down as lumps of coal.

It was unbelievable that neither Neil nor Mark seemed to notice how stilted the exchanges were between the two women—Mark in particular as he was normally so astute.

'You're a wonderful cook,' Ginny said tightly, after a particularly long silence. 'Mark's very lucky.'

'How about telling *him* that?' grated Sarah, equally tightly.

Mark lowered his knife and fork, the resignation in his expression telling Ginny he hadn't been as oblivious to the atmosphere as he'd pretended. 'I'll help you with dessert,' he told Sarah wearily. 'Ginny, change the music.'

When they left the room Ginny avoided Neil's puzzled eyes, too bewildered herself to want to talk about the evening with him. She left the table and flicked slowly through Sarah's sizeable collection of CDs.

If this hostility was all about her and Neil, interrupting their love-making, then Sarah was being unreasonable, she decided. They hadn't turned up uninvited.

The sudden blare of Neil's bleeper came as a welcome relief to the silence and Ginny listened to his conversation when he telephoned, gathering that he was needed at the hospital to see a patient urgently.

'Sorry,' he said, replacing the receiver. 'I won't be able to drop you home.'

Ginny was already collecting her handbag. 'I'll get a cab from the hospital,' she said briskly. She had no intention of being left here without him and it was a good excuse to leave early. She couldn't imagine their hostess raising any objections to her departure.

But Mark had come to the door. 'No, I'll drive you,' he said grimly, his gaze darkly determined, ignoring the frantic way she was shaking her head. 'You go on, Neil. I want to take Ginny home.'

# CHAPTER THREE

DESPITE Ginny's determination to escape immediately, Neil provided no help at all, obviously distracted by the phone call and grateful for Mark's offer, leaving Ginny frustrated and feeling vaguely like an unwanted package. He kissed her cheek, waved his thanks to Mark and asked them to be passed on to Sarah, and within seconds had gone.

Mark said evenly, 'Dessert's off. Give me a few minutes and we'll leave.' He closed the door to the kitchen again, leaving her alone.

When he reappeared he was pulling on his coat and Ginny peered doubtfully behind him. 'Shouldn't I thank Sarah?'

'She's not well,' he said tightly, ushering her towards the door and out into the misty damp night air. 'A headache. I've told her to go to bed. She sends her apologies.'

She waited until they were a mile or so away from the house. 'Mark, have I offended Sarah in some way?'

'No.' He didn't look at her, his attention on the inter-section ahead.

'She doesn't like me very much.'

His eyes flickered briefly to her face. 'She hardly knows you.'

'She definitely didn't want me there tonight.'

'You're over-sensitive.'

'And you're deliberately obtuse!' Sure now that he was concealing something, Ginny found herself annoyed. 'This would be easier if you told me the truth. If I don't know what I've done wrong I can't do anything about it.'

Mark slowed then braked for a set of traffic lights and

she thought he was going to ignore her, but he said, 'Sarah wasn't herself tonight.'

'So I gathered,' Ginny snapped. Although, in truth, she and Sarah had never got on particularly well, this was certainly the first time there'd ever been any overt hostility.

'I'm sure she'll call tomorrow and apologise.'

'She doesn't need to do that,' Ginny said quickly, not wanting an awkwardly embarrassing conversation like that at all. Backtracking, she stammered, 'T-tell her I understand. I know what it's like when you get a bad headache. You're right, I am a little over-sensitive sometimes. I shouldn't even have mentioned anything—'

The shrill sound of Mark's mobile made her start and Ginny fell silent while Mark pulled abruptly off into a lay-by, sparing her only a brief glance as he hauled the phone out of his jacket. 'Mark Reynolds,' he said tersely.

She heard Donald's voice, and caught a few words, inculding 'emergency' and 'ambulance'.

Mark said, 'I'm almost at the surgery now. I'll pick up our monitor and check things out.' He dumped the phone onto Ginny's lap and accelerated out onto the road, then turned right into the practice's street. 'Donald's swamped. One of his patients who lives in the village called about some chest pain,' he told her. 'Thinks it's indigestion but Donald says he's stalwart so he's worried. He wanted to send an ambulance directly but the man refuses any fuss. I can drop you off on the way.'

'It'll take too long.' Ginny opened her door as he stopped outside the surgery. 'I'll get the cardiac kit.'

'According to Donald, no heart or peptic history,' he told her as they pulled up in front of a brick, terraced flat a few minutes later. He rapped at the green wooden door and when there was no reply they both peered through a side window. A corner lamp revealed a tidy sitting room, but no patient.

Mark thumped at the door again and jangled the metal cover over the letter slot. 'Mr Gates, it's the doctors.'

Still no reply. They exchanged tense looks then Mark stepped back and they briefly inspected the block, which stretched at least six flats in each direction. 'No time to run around to the back,' he said tightly. He braced himself and charged into the door with his shoulder, splintering the lock enough for a second blow to force the door open.

They found Mr Gates slumped in a chair in the kitchen. A middle-aged man with a craggy grey face, he lifted his head weakly as they charged in and rasped, 'Sorry. Couldn't move. Pain...'

'We'll help with that.' Mark eased him from the chair to the rug, and lifted his plaid shirt. Ginny placed a monitor lead at each clammy shoulder and one beneath his heart.

Eyeing the trace, Mark reached for an ampoule of diamorphine, then some metoclopramide. 'The pain's coming from your heart.' He waited while Ginny swiftly inserted a Venflon into Mr Gates's arm then moved forward and injected the painkiller. 'This will help but you'll have to go to hospital.'

Mr Gates's weak nod suggested he understood.

Ginny handed Mark a bottle of GTN spray and an aspirin, before reaching for the telephone on the bench behind them and ordering an ambulance. 'Mark, there's a run of ventriculars,' she said urgently, when three wide, irregular beats appeared on the monitor.

'I see them.' Mark was checking Mr Gates's blood pressure. 'One-ten over eighty. Not bad. We'll hold off for now but he might need some lignocaine.'

'Lignocaine ready.' Ginny drew up an ampoule. Their patient was still pale and possibly more sweaty than earlier. 'How's the pain, Mr Gates?'

'Better,' he said weakly, 'but I feel strange...' As he let himself lie back on the floor Ginny saw two more irregular beats, then his rhythm strip changed to irregular chaos and he sagged into unconsciousness.

'V-fib,' she said crisply, ripping open a pair of pads while the defibrillator charged. 'Clear.' She shocked him.

'Still V-fib,' said Mark. 'Shock again.'

'Clear.'

'No change.' Mark inserted an airway and gave four quick breaths, then commenced cardiac compressions. 'Try increasing the voltage.'

'Three-sixty,' she confirmed, waiting for the machine to recharge. 'Clear.'

'Sinus.' Mark grinned approval as their patient took a deep shuddering breath. He lowered his head and pumped up the blood-pressure cuff. 'Still one-ten over eighty. More ectopics. Try the lignocaine.'

'Loading one hundred.' Ginny settled herself on the ground so she could push the drug slowly into the Venflon. 'All right, Mr Gates?'

'Hmm?' His eyes blinked slowly open. 'I think so,' he said hoarsely. 'Is that the ambulance?'

'Your hearing's better than mine,' Ginny said a few seconds later, only just able to pick up the faint siren over the sound of her heart, pounding in her ears. 'It should be yours, yes.'

He clutched at her hand. 'Will I be away long?' he rasped. 'Only my son and his family's coming to visit. I like to have the place nice.'

'You'll probably be in hospital around ten days,' she said gently.

'And your son would rather see you well, even if it means you're in hospital,' Mark said firmly, his tone allowing no argument, as the ambulance drew up outside.

The paramedics loaded Mr Gates onto a trolley and one of them grinned at the splintered front door as they wheeled him outside. 'Play a bit of rugby, do you?' he asked Ginny teasingly.

'My partner played at varsity,' she confirmed, returning his grin with wry acknowledgement that there was no way she could have smashed her way inside. It was lucky for all of them that Mark had been here tonight.

'We'll let the local police know,' the ambulance officer said. 'They'll make sure everything's secured.'

Mark appeared with their equipment as Mr Gates was being loaded into the ambulance. 'I'll go with them,' Mark told her as he stacked the cardiac box into his boot. 'Just in case. You may as well take my car home and pick me up at the house in the morning.'

However, experience had taught Ginny that he might have to wait hours for a lift back to the village so she followed the ambulance into Norwich and collected him from outside Casualty.

'I thought you were going home,' he said, opening the door and waiting for her to shift across to the passenger seat.

'You mean you thought you told me to go home,' she countered. She swivelled her legs over the console in the middle of the car. 'There wasn't any point. I'm so full of adrenaline I wouldn't have slept anyway.'

'Real medicine,' he said, almost mockingly. He fastened his seat belt. 'Like being in hospital again. Fun, isn't it?'

'Now and again.' Ginny held up hands which still trembled faintly. 'I don't miss hospital work, though. Do you?'

'Sometimes.' He indicated, then turned out of the hospital car park. 'I like the instant rewards of hospital practice.'

'You like the action.' She smiled. 'You always did. Even after all these years part of me is still surprised you chose general practice.'

'At times I wonder if the reasons weren't more subcon-

scious than conscious,' he acknowledged, meeting her surprised look with a calm one of his own. 'Not that I don't
enjoy what I do,' he continued.

'And soon you'll be teaching,' she added huskily, avoiding his eyes to stare out into the blurred, streetlamp-lit darkness. 'That'll be a change.'

There was a long silence, then Mark said, 'Ginny, about
dinner tonight, I'm sorry.' At her sharp look he added,
'Sorry about what happened with Sarah.'

Ginny tensed. 'She wasn't feeling well—'

'Sarah's uneasy about you,' Mark said abruptly. 'About
you and me. She doesn't understand.'

'Oh.' She lowered her head. 'I didn't realise.'

'It's not as if it hasn't happened before.'

No, it wasn't, she thought wearily, averting her eyes
from the dazzle of oncoming headlights. If Sarah was jealous of her relationship with Mark, it explained everything
although, given how long the geriatrician had been dating
Mark, it wasn't so surprising she hadn't considered it.

In the past some of Mark's girlfriends had been suspicious of her, but while Mark had generally found that amus-
ing, Ginny, for his sake, had always made an effort to reassure them that she and Mark were merely friends and
colleagues. With Sarah she hadn't been aware that there
had been any need for that. She moistened her lips.
'Should…should I say something to her?'

'No!' Mark spoke harshly. At her startled look he added
more calmly, 'No. Believe me, that wouldn't be a good
idea.'

'But you've explained—'

'Of course I have.' He changed lanes to overtake a slow-
moving lorry, waiting until he was back on the left before
continuing, 'But until tonight I didn't realise the problem
wasn't resolved.'

'But we've never—'

'You and I know that, but who else believes it?' He sounded impatient and the brief assessing glance that encompassed her tensely held frame and dropped to the narrow line of her legs beneath her skirt was irritable, almost annoyed. 'You're an intelligent, sexy, beautiful woman. We've been together almost every day for more than a decade. Sometimes I find it hard to believe myself.'

Ginny's mouth had dropped open at the 'sexy' and now she gasped. 'But we're friends!'

'Which makes it stranger.'

Mark changed down for the roundabout and she looked away abruptly, watching the trees flash by as he accelerated onto the dual carriageway. 'Sarah sounds very insecure,' she said quietly, struggling to keep her tone neutral. 'You obviously need to work harder at convincing her about your feelings.'

'Why do you think you and I never had an affair?'

'Th-the issue never arose.' She refused to look at him, her eyes fixed on the windscreen. 'I guess in the beginning something might have happened, but…well, we became friends and our friendship's obviously important to both of us.' She folded her arms nervously. 'Besides, there was always so much work to do to have time for much else.' She flushed. 'And it's not as if you've ever lacked female attention. That probably made our friendship seem more valuable.'

Hurriedly she added, 'After med school, after we formed the practice, I suppose our partnership was too important to risk by changing anything.'

'You've given this some thought.'

'A little.' Much of it was a rehearsed speech she normally had to deliver every time she went out with anyone. Given that Mark's girlfriends tended to be suspicious of her, it was hardly surprising that the few men she'd dated over the years had felt threatened by Mark.

'Sarah says you'd be easier to accept if you *were* actually an old girlfriend.'

Ginny kept the fact that she thought Sarah was sounding more and more pathetic to herself. 'She doesn't have to accept me,' she said coolly. 'You and I don't come as a package.'

'Until now we have.'

'Well, that's about to change.' She saw his mouth compress and frowned at him. 'Isn't it? Isn't that what dinner tonight was all about? The big announcement?'

They were approaching the village now. She could see the haze of orange light and he slowed, staring at her. 'What big announcement?'

'The engagement,' she said brittlely. 'Or the move, whatever. I saw the fridge, Mark. It was full of champagne. What went wrong? Was Sarah so annoyed at seeing your arm around me that she called it off?'

'Would that please you?'

'Me?' She blinked at him. 'This has nothing to do with me.'

'Hasn't it?'

'You're talking in riddles.' She lifted a weary hand to shield her eyes, feeling the car turn into her street. 'Of course I don't want you to go, but I also want you to be happy.'

He drew up outside her flat. 'Sarah believes that the reason for my difficulties, deciding whether or not to go to Scotland, is that I don't want to leave you.'

'Well...we're friends as well as business partners,' she ventured. 'I don't want you to go either—'

'She means that I don't want to leave you because our relationship is unresolved,' he interjected. 'I'm not talking about friendship, Ginny, I'm talking about sex.' His mouth tightened. 'Or, more appropriately in this case, *lack* of sex.'

She recoiled. 'But th-that's absurd,' she stammered,

shaking her head wildly. And it was. Sarah had obviously said things to him which were completely distorting his understanding of their relationship. 'Surely you don't believe that?'

He didn't move. 'There's one very easy way to find out.'

She gasped. 'No!'

'Because you're in love with Neil?'

'Of course not.' She fumbled for the doorcatch. 'Sarah's mad!' She thrust open her door and scrambled out. 'You're both mad. Go home, Mark. Get some sleep. You must be over-tired.'

She slammed the door but before she reached the flat he'd opened his own and climbed out, leaning against the roof of the car as he watched her fumble for her keys. 'Gin...?'

Reluctantly she returned his gaze, glad that it was too dark for him to see that her face was the colour of beetroot. 'What?'

'You were great tonight,' he said softly. 'That resuscitation was perfect. There's no one else I'd rather work with.'

'Thank you.' She stared at him and it felt as if she'd been winded. 'I feel the same about you.'

For a few seconds they just looked at each other, then Mark ducked his head, returned to the driver's seat and left her.

An hour later Ginny was wandering restlessly around her flat, drenched in guilt, unable to settle, asking herself again and again how she could have run from him like that. What sort of friend was she? Clearly he and Sarah were having problems and tonight he'd wanted to talk to her, had started to confide Sarah's feelings and his own, clearly confused reaction to them but, instead of listening as she should have, she'd panicked and deserted him.

She felt awful. For years Mark had acted as a sounding-board for her problems, but it was extraordinarily rare for him to turn to her with problems in his personal life. Tonight, when he had, she hadn't even tried to understand.

If she'd listened to him properly, taken the time to make him see that Sarah's accusations were simply the product of her misguided jealousy and had no rational basis, they would have resolved the issue immediately with no harm. By now they'd be laughing hysterically about that conversation.

Knowing she'd never settle without making some attempt to resolve this, she collected her keys. She doubted whether Mark would have heeded her advice to take an early night, but if there were no lights visible at the house she'd simply turn around and drive home.

However, when she arrived she saw that the kitchen lights were still on and so she ran up to his door. She'd not brought her jacket and the cold air made goose-bumps form on her bare arms. Rather than waiting for him to come to the door, she used her own key to let herself into the welcoming warmth of his home.

'Mark, it's me…'

Mark, bare-chested but still wearing the pants he'd had on earlier, was speaking on the telephone. He whirled to see her. The soft lighting made it hard to read his expression accurately, but he was obviously startled and Ginny hesitated. Clearly he hadn't heard her car outside on the gravel, as she'd assumed. She mouthed an apology then pointed to the door, asking in mime if he wanted her to leave.

Mark shook his head, frowning slightly. 'You've been under a lot of strain,' he said soothingly to the person he was speaking to, his darkly shadowed eyes on Ginny, 'but tranquillisers aren't the solution.'

Ginny felt a rush of fondness for him, not surprised that he was talking with one of his patients. Even when he wasn't on call it would be typical of Mark to tell people he was concerned about to call him directly.

She waited a few minutes in case he finished, her gaze fluttering between the muted Constable print on the cream wall beside him and the less familiar, muscled shape of Mark's chest and shoulders. He was extraordinarily attractive, she acknowledged, not appreciating the reminder after their disturbing conversation earlier. No wonder Sarah was possessive. Being in love with a man with Mark's appeal couldn't be easy.

Her eyes flickered up and her face prickled with heat as she realised he'd caught her looking at him.

'One bottle of wine doesn't make you an alcoholic,' he said, his eyes not moving from Ginny, 'but you know as well as I do that alcohol won't help.'

She widened her eyes at him enquiringly but his regard didn't falter. Unable to sustain the contact, she dropped her gaze again and shifted her weight from one foot to the other.

Perhaps he'd rather she didn't listen to his conversation. But when she ducked around the wall, separating the living and eating areas, into the kitchen he moved too. He opened the door beside him and turned so that he looked into the kitchen, still watching her.

Thinking he might simply have been being polite earlier, she pointed to herself once more and mimed leaving, but Mark frowned and bounced his palm towards the floor to indicate that she should stay.

Trying to shrug off her self-consciousness, Ginny started to prepare coffee for them, but even with her back to him she could feel his eyes on her. Deciding not to grind fresh beans as the noise would disturb his conversation, she spooned instant coffee into the two cups she'd laid out, but her hands were cold and shaky and she spilled some of the granules.

'What about seeing a therapist?' he asked. Apparently his patient didn't agree with that suggestion because Mark's next comment was, 'No, in all honesty, I don't think you're better off, talking to me.'

Ginny turned and smiled sympathetically but Mark didn't return her smile. If anything, his eyes darkened, and she twisted away hastily and stared fixedly at the kettle, willing it to boil, wondering what on earth was wrong with her— with both of them.

Mark continued to soothe his patient and when the water was finally ready Ginny snatched the kettle off its base, managing to splash the underside of her wrist with some of the scalding liquid. Swearing under her breath, she ran her hand under fast, cold water and grimaced at the faint pink mark that demarcated the burn.

More carefully, she finished pouring and when she carried one cup to Mark she mouthed, 'Instant. Sorry.'

Instead of accepting the coffee, Mark transferred the cup to the table beside him and reached for her hand. 'I understand what you're saying,' he said, his dark, brooding gaze locked with Ginny's. Abruptly he lifted her hand and pressed his mouth to her sore wrist.

For a few taut seconds neither of them moved, then Ginny gasped. She snatched her hand away and backed until she came up against his marble bench. Shaking, she spun and braced her arms against the cool stone. The touch of his mouth to her flesh, although brief, had been the gesture of a lover, but it hadn't been abhorrent—far from it.

Dimly through the buzz of her own confusion she heard a series of monosyllabic replies and realised that Mark's conversation was ending. There was the sound of the receiver being lowered then nothing until she felt the strong heat of his hands on her shoulders as he turned her around.

'Mark, what are you doing?'

'Shut up, Gin.' Before she could react he kissed her,

kissed her properly—a hard, passionate, searing kiss that turned her world upside down.

'No—'

He lifted his head and his face was flushed and his eyes dark and brilliant. 'Then why are you here?'

She twisted her head free, appalled. 'You wanted to talk.'

'I don't want to talk, I want *you*.' He was breathing as fast as she was. 'Here. Now. Right now.'

'But that's absurd. We can't possibly…'

'Because of Neil?'

'No!'

'Then why not?' His demand was urgent, impatient, and she felt as if she were drowning. 'We're both adults, both capable of deciding what we want.'

'Mark, we're not…we've never… This is crazy.'

'Tell me to stop,' he rasped. 'Tell me to stop and I will.'

She opened her mouth, meaning to say the words, but nothing came out. She did want him, she realised helplessly. It was wrong and it was insane and the list of reasons why she shouldn't was endless, but it didn't change how she felt and she'd never felt anything like this need before and it was filling her up and she didn't know what to do.

For a few brief seconds there was silence then Mark muttered a harsh imprecation and reached for her—and she let him. He twisted her and backed her against the bench, his hands at the fastenings of her top. Astonishingly, as she'd never behaved that way in her life, her voice urged him on while her breath flew harsh and raw in and out of her aching chest.

She felt him disentangle her hands then slide the linen shirt from her shoulders, but she was too busy with his mouth to worry when he tugged down the soft thermal teddy which was the only thing hiding her breasts from him. She felt dizzy. Passion, she supposed dimly, overwhelmed.

He tipped her back and his mouth was warm and damp and teasing at her breasts. Unconsciously she arched, delighting in the arousal evident against her thighs. His mouth on her felt so good that her hands acted of their own accord and gripped his hair, holding him to her so that even if he'd wanted to he couldn't have pulled away.

She gasped when his palms slid up under her skirt and gripped her buttocks, lifting her against him. Ignoring her faint protest, his mouth shifted from her breasts to her throat then to her mouth, which welcomed him greedily. His voice was hoarse against her ear. 'Let me, Gin.'

She twisted so their mouths met again, the embrace fierce and hungry. Don't stop, she wanted to say, but she couldn't spare the energy for words. Instead, she guided his head back to her breasts, rejoicing in the soft groan that told her he wasn't going to pull away.

When he lifted his head next his face was flushed and his eyes glittering. He lowered her feet to the floor for a brief moment and she clung to him frantically, her nails gripping his hard flesh, but he wasn't resisting her. Their gazes melded, their chests lifting with the effort of drawing breath. He stripped his clothes in a few brief and precise movements, then released her skirt and roughly pulled away her underwear and tights, dropping them onto the floor with his clothes before lifting her back onto the bench.

She gasped as he entered her, the impact knocking her back so it was only the fierceness of her grasp on the edge of the marble that kept her upright, but there was no discomfort. Her body accepted him with a smooth, aching liquidity and she folded her legs around him, gripping his thighs with her heels as he thrust again, altering the angle so the movement was perfectly adjusted to the needs of her body.

She twisted her head from side to side, her eyes tightly closed, then became still so there was only his movement as she concentrated on the astonishing pressure building within her. Then she twisted, shifted, as the pressure became unbearable and there was only him and this and his mouth at her breast and his voice, urging her closer and harder.

'Please…' Her eyes closed tightly. 'Mark, don't stop…'

As if her voice inflamed him he gripped her harder, forcing their bodies even closer, his face buried between her breasts.

She might have screamed at the end, she wasn't sure, but he was silent, the only outward sign of his pleasure the momentary rigidity of his muscles and the harsh breaths that followed.

He held her still for a minute, perhaps two, while their breaths calmed but then pulled back, not allowing any languid dénouement to soften his withdrawal. Suddenly Ginny knew herself again and she was cold, icily cold. She shivered, then slowly opened her eyes. What she saw, she imagined, mirrored her own expression—stark, unmitigated shock.

God! What had they done?

She felt sick. Pushing him aside, she slid from the bench, stumbled upstairs to his bathroom and pulled the door shut behind her. As suddenly as it had come, the nausea retreated and she sank onto the edge of the bath and stared at the tiled wall, shivering, numb, appalled.

Eventually there was a tap on the door. 'Ginny?' She raised her head, her eyes on the handle, but it didn't move. 'Are you…all right?' His voice sounded strained.

'Yes.' Her voice cracked and she grimaced at the absurdity of the word. She straightened, wiping her face. 'I'm fine. I'll be out in a minute.'

'I've collected your clothes. They're outside the door.'

Ginny waited for him to leave, before opening the door. She snatched up the clothes—her crumpled linen top and skirt, together with her underwear—threw her laddered tights into the bin then dressed quickly but shakily, her fingers fumbling, twice having to redo the fastening of the top because she'd matched the wrong buttons with the wrong holes.

She found him on the sofa downstairs, fully dressed, his head buried in his hands. He'd obviously not heard her approach and she hesitated in the doorway. 'Mark...?'

His head snapped up and she caught her breath at the dazed expression she glimpsed before the shutters came down. 'So, what happens now?' he said heavily.

She curled her fingers around the wooden doorframe for support. 'I—I don't know.' Her voice sounded like the rasping of sandpaper. She needed him to hug her, comfort her, tell her that they'd made a mistake but that it hadn't changed anything and that they could forget it. Instead, he was cold and distant and she knew that everything had changed. She felt lost. 'What do you think?'

'That we're both tired.' He sounded tired. Tired, and as stunned as she herself felt. 'Are you staying?'

It was a simple question and one he'd asked many times. He'd leaned back and his eyes were closed and he wasn't even looking at her, but suddenly Ginny's body felt tight and awkward and her face burned.

The silence stretched and she still couldn't answer. Finally he opened his eyes and looked directly at her. His gaze was very dark and she didn't know what she wanted to say but she opened her mouth and the words stumbled out. 'I want to go home.'

'I'll take you.' His expression shuttered, he stood. 'You can't drive.'

She lowered her head in acquiescence. He was right about that—she was barely managing to stand.

Neither of them spoke on the short drive to her flat and the atmosphere inside the Audi was tense and uncomfortable. As soon as he stopped in front of her building she climbed out stiffly and went directly up the steps to her door. Once inside her flat she waited until she heard him drive away then sank silently to the floor.

# CHAPTER FOUR

THREE hours later Ginny pulled herself out of the chair in which she'd been sitting, showered, dressed and walked to the surgery. She spent the hour while it was quiet catching up on routine paperwork that didn't require her to think of anything beyond the mechanical process of transferring details from the computer to paper. By the time the rest of the staff started arriving for eight she'd drunk enough coffee to give herself a caffeine buzz which she hoped would sustain her through the day.

Friday morning's clinic included a lot of her antenatal patients and obstetric follow-ups, and even with the help of their community midwife and Lynn it was always busy. Still, Ginny loved seeing her pregnant patients. There was often a special serenity about women during late pregnancy and, considering how tightly coiled her nerves were this morning, the gentle act of examining a pregnant abdomen and listening quietly for the rapid fluttering of an unborn baby's tiny heart was therapeutic.

Her last patient of the morning, a twenty-five-year-old woman, Michelle Parker, was in the thirty-third week of her first pregnancy. Lynn drew her attention to the trace of protein in Michelle's urine. There were no other signs of pre-eclampsia—a complication of pregnancy which, untreated, could cause seizures. Her blood pressure was normal and she had no pitting oedema in her legs, but Ginny preferred to be cautious.

'I want you to see Lynn on Monday to have your blood pressure checked again,' she said firmly. 'In the meantime, call me immediately if your legs or hands or feet start to swell. We'll send this urine to the laboratory for urgent analysis. They'll check to see if there's any infection present and give us a preliminary result tomorrow afternoon. We'll phone you if you need to pick up a prescription.'

Michelle said, 'But I feel well. I don't have any burning or stinging.'

'Not all infections cause symptoms,' Ginny explained, 'and infections are easy to pick up in pregnancy because the hormones mean your plumbing's more relaxed than normal so it's easier for the bacteria to get into the system. If there's anything like that present it's important we treat it quickly because there's always a very small risk an infection might bring on labour prematurely.'

She mustered a reassuring smile. 'But you're fit, your scans are good, baby's very active and he or she has a terrifically strong heartbeat. There's every reason to expect a completely normal delivery.'

'Natural delivery,' Michelle said firmly. 'I want a natural delivery. No injections or painkillers or anything like that.'

Ginny squeezed her arm as she walked her to the door. Most of her patients these days expressed that wish or even the desire to deliver without any hospital intervention at all. Although she acknowledged the mothers' rights to make those decisions, Ginny's training had been conservative and she still worried about the rare occasions when that wouldn't be in the best interests of mother or baby.

'Keep a tiny corner of your mind open,' she said gently, making a mental note to discuss the issue with Michelle again nearer the time. In her experience, mothers who had their minds fixed rigidly on a natural delivery, with no acknowledgement that medication was sometimes needed for either their own or their baby's sakes, tended to feel as if they'd failed when labour or delivery didn't go strictly to plan.

Thinking of things going wrong brought Ginny right

back to Mark again and the dizzy, sick feeling of dread which had been lurking in her abdomen all morning. What was she going to say to him? What about his relationship with Sarah? How could she possibly have behaved like that? How could *either* of them have behaved like that?

The rumble of his voice in the corridor brought her head up sharply, but he didn't open her door and she started breathing again when she heard the side door close and realised he'd left for his house calls.

That afternoon Lynn told her that he'd cancelled his customary Friday half-day to do paperwork, but by six she still hadn't seen him. Sure now that he was just as keen to avoid her as she was him, she relaxed a little. Then there was a brief knock and Mark was there, his expression carefully neutral. 'I'll give you a lift to collect your car.'

'Fine,' she said stiffly. In her distraction she'd forgotten she had no transport and as she was on call now she needed it. 'Give me a few minutes. I'll meet you outside.'

He nodded and closed the door behind him.

Ginny dipped her head, her eyes closed, and took three long, slow breaths. She clicked her bag closed, grabbed her coat from the rack and left the office.

He didn't say anything when she joined him in the car and Ginny shifted uneasily as he drove through the village and the silence began to stretch. 'This morning was nice,' she said huskily, 'but it's turned rather cool again, hasn't it?'

'God, Ginny, let's not start talking about the weather.'

She swallowed. 'I guess it was a silly thing to say,' she conceded. When he didn't reply she cleared her throat. 'Have you...have you said anything to Sarah about...last night?'

She saw his fingers tighten on the steering-wheel. 'Have you told Neil?'

'There's no reason to.' She was tired of correcting him

about her relationship with Neil and now she didn't bother. She couldn't stop the guilt they were both experiencing about Sarah but she vowed to try and lessen its impact on their lives. 'Mark, you and Sarah aren't married yet and as she's already a bit jealous...well, if I were her I think I'd rather not know anything about last night.'

'Come off it.' He sounded exasperated. 'I know you much better than that, Gin. You'd demand to know everything. Every little intimate detail.'

'No!'

'You're just worried there'll be a fuss if she finds out.'

'That's not fair.'

'Isn't it?' He swung into his drive, parked beside her car, then turned off the engine with an abruptness that betrayed his frustration. He opened his door but didn't get out, his eyes veiled as he swivelled towards her. 'Relax,' he said wearily. 'I'm not going to tell Sarah anything. There's no reason to. What happened was the result of a...combination of circumstances. It's nobody's business but ours.'

'I think that's the most sensible attitude.' Relief drained the tension from her fists and they loosened, fiddling at the strap of her bag. Wondering what he meant exactly by 'combination of circumstances' but too wary of provoking a response she wasn't ready to deal with yet, she said instead, 'I realise you must be feeling guilty—'

'What's this, Ginny? Transference or projection?'

Her head snapped up and she flushed at his abrupt mockery. 'I'm sure we're *both* feeling guilty,' she said tightly. She was also guilty of both psychological devices of which he'd accused her but that didn't mean she wasn't right. 'But Sarah shouldn't suffer because of one stupid mistake—'

'Are we talking about Sarah or are we talking about Neil?' Before she could say anything he said harshly, 'Forget it. Either way, it doesn't matter.' He opened her door and looked pointedly at her car. 'You'd better go. I don't think either of us is in the right sort of mood to discuss this now.'

She swallowed heavily. 'Mark, you don't understand. I'm thinking of you—'

'Then don't.' He thrust his fingers through his hair. 'I'm sorry, Gin. Not now. Let it rest, hmm?'

'All right.' She understood that he needed more time. She did, too. A lot more time. Her hands shook as she fumbled at her handbag. As she riffled through it her movements became increasingly jerky. 'I can't find my keys,' she said thickly. 'They're not here.'

Mark levered himself out of the car. 'Tip it out.'

She upended the bag onto his seat and sifted through the muddled contents. It was months since she'd gone through it last and it was cluttered. Her purse, cheque-book, credit cards, some tissues, contraceptive pills, a pen, a few ancient scribbled shopping lists and receipts and scraps of paper and lipsticks tumbled out, but no keys. She gathered them all back into her bag, casting him a despairing look. 'See? Not there. I must have left them at home.'

Mark glanced at the house. 'Or inside,' he countered. 'You might have left them on the hall table when you let yourself in last night. I don't remember you carrying them home.' He strode around. 'Come and look.'

Ginny's face stiffened. She knew it was pathetic but she didn't want to go in to his house right now. She didn't need any reminder of the night before. 'I'll wait out here,' she said huskily.

From his sudden stillness she knew he was remembering just as she was remembering. 'Fine,' he said tightly. 'Stay in the car. It's warmer.'

She flinched at the slam of the door then watched him walk towards the house, hating the way her eyes lingered involuntarily on the tight strength of his long legs. Given the formality between them, it was hard to believe that less than twenty-four hours earlier they'd been locked together in the most intimate embrace possible.

Ginny leaned her head against the back of her seat, wiped her face and groaned. Well, at least it would have been hard to believe if the imagery of him against her wasn't so vivid every time she closed her eyes that she feared it had been seared into her brain.

He was only gone a few minutes. He held out the dangling keys so she could see he had them then walked directly to her car and unlocked it. He stood aside, not saying anything while she climbed in awkwardly, and by the time she'd started the car and backed it around he'd gone.

On Monday morning Ginny was at the surgery before seven again, and as she sorted through the night claim forms she'd been organising she reflected grimly that at least some good might come from the disaster of the week before. One or two more marathon sessions of paperwork like the weekend she'd just had and for the first time in years she might be up to date.

Mark arrived at eight and she stiffened, staring at her door, but after greeting the receptionist she heard him go directly to his office.

Just before two she steeled herself to go and find him. He was in the clinical room, suturing a toddler's cut forehead. After smiling weakly at Lynn, who was assisting him by keeping the child soothed, Ginny waited until he'd tied his final, precise knot to say anything.

'If it's all right with you, I'll take my half-day.'

'Fine.' His head bent over his work as he applied a small dressing and then stuck a little gold star to his patient's tiny hand as a reward for being so good, barely acknowledging her.

'Did you...have a good weekend?'

The husky words brought his head up. His dark gaze

flicked briefly to Lynn, who'd turned away and was sorting his instruments, then back to Ginny, making her flustered. 'Did you?'

She lifted one shoulder doubtfully. 'I got lots of paper-work done.'

His eyes narrowed. 'Conscientious of you.'

Lynn grinned as she lifted their patient from the table for a cuddle. To Ginny's relief, she was busy admiring the child's shiny star, and apparently hadn't noticed how awkward and stilted their exchange had been. 'Miles will be rubbing his hands together,' she chirped, referring to their practice manager. 'From the size of that load you brought in this morning you must have done a few months work yourself, Mark.'

Ginny looked at him quickly—she'd assumed he'd be spending the weekend with Sarah—but he avoided her questioning gaze. 'How's the list this afternoon?' he asked Lynn, turning away from Ginny to scrub his hands. It made her feel excluded but at the same time drew her reluctant attention to the strength of his shoulders as he bent over the basin—hard, broad shoulders, covered by smooth, warm skin she'd driven her nails into.

'Your list is massive.' Lynn clucked at her little patient approvingly. 'Come on, cutie. Let's find Mummy for you.' She grinned at Ginny again. 'Sure Mark can't persuade you to stay and give us a hand?'

Ginny stiffened. She looked at Mark. 'I have to go—'

'I don't need any help—'

They both spoke at the same time and Ginny bit her lip and flushed, reading his gaze effortlessly. He wanted her assistance as little as she felt capable of giving it. Often she did work an hour or so later on a Monday if his clinic was large, but that meant working closely with Mark and she was too jumpy to manage that today.

'I can cope,' Mark said firmly.

Lynn gave him a strange look but shrugged. 'Whatever,' she said easily. 'You're the boss.'

'You're busy.' Ginny held out slightly shaky arms for the toddler and relieved Lynn of the wriggling load. 'Yes, it's a beautiful star, darling. What does Mum look like?'

'Small with red hair.' Lynn smiled her thanks. 'Bye.'

Ginny didn't see Mark at all the following day as they kept missing each other. She was out on calls much of the morning, he took lunch after her clinic started and he was out on calls when it finished.

They were busy people, she rationalised, but inwardly she knew that there was more than her cowardice keeping them apart. In five years of general practice together they'd always made time to meet during the day. Knowing that Mark was avoiding her as much as she was him wasn't any comfort at all. Sooner or later they'd have to talk. Talk properly. And the longer they waited the worse it would be.

On Wednesday Ginny arrived back at the surgery only a little late from her afternoon calls to find the surgery deserted, the car park empty and the building locked. Surprised, but relieved that Mark had already gone, she let herself in then froze, startled by the balloon that brushed her face.

'Surprise!' Lynn rushed across and kissed her cheek and Ginny blinked in puzzlement at the rest of the staff and Neil as they appeared from the other offices, bearing gifts. 'You didn't say a word all day,' Lynn chided. 'Did you think we'd forgotten?'

Ginny stared at them all, bemused. 'I—I should have known better,' she stammered finally. 'Minds like elephants, you lot.' She met Mark's shrewdly knowing look with a flush. He understood exactly how she could have forgotten the significance of the date. 'Thank you, every-body.'

Neil popped a bottle of champagne, then leaned forward to kiss her cheek. 'Happy birthday,' he said lightly, adding more quietly, 'Lynn invited me. You don't mind?'

Conscious of Mark's dark stare, she returned Neil's kiss more warmly than she might have normally. 'On the contrary. I'm glad you could come.' She accepted a drink and took several steadying sips. 'Cheers.'

'Presents, then cake,' ordered Lynn, taking control. 'Ginny, look at Neil's first because he has to run away to give a lecture.'

Ginny opened the packet he gave her with a smile which was still slightly shaky, but it strengthened when she revealed a pair of thick woollen gloves.

'I remembered you lost yours,' he said sheepishly.

Ginny kissed him again. 'They'll be good in winter.'

'Have some of my strawberry shortcake, you romantic.' As Lynn passed him a plate she rolled her eyes expressively at Ginny and mouthed, 'Men!'

Miles, their manager, had bought her a huge bunch of spring flowers, and by the time she'd put them in water and unwrapped the sunlit water-colour of the village square, which the staff had joined together to buy, Neil as well as Miles had to leave. She went with Neil out to the car he'd parked discreetly along the street, then returned to find the nurses hanging the picture in place of her obstetrics diploma in her office.

Lynn beamed. 'Like it?'

'I love it. Much more interesting.' Her smile faltered slightly as her gaze met Mark's. 'Thank you, everybody. My turn for cake?'

'Open Mark's present,' Lynn said. 'Stop pretending you didn't get her anything,' she scolded him. 'We all know you'd never forget.'

After a hesitation so brief she suspected she was the only one to notice he held out a small parcel and Ginny took it, knowing she was flushing. Not looking at him, she unfastened the paper carefully, opened the blue felt box and gazed down at the gold bracelet which nestled inside.

One of the receptionists looked over her shoulder. 'Oh, it's gorgeous.' Close enough to see the engraving, she said, '"For G"', it says. Isn't that lovely?'

'Lovely,' Ginny echoed huskily, suddenly on the brink of tears.

'It matches the chain you bought her for Christmas.' Lynn sounded awed. 'Come on, Ginny. Try it on. It's beautiful.'

'Yes.' Ginny lifted out the flat band. Not expecting it to be so heavy—and concentrating on keeping her eyes dry—she fumbled with the warm gold bracelet, and Mark took it from her hand.

While she stood very still he undid the clasp and fastened the bracelet around her wrist. While the others oohed and aahed over the gift his thumb lingered for one soft, breathtaking moment beneath the gold and on the skin she'd burned that night at his home.

Her eyes flew to his face but his expression was unreadable. 'Th-thank you.'

'Donald's practice sent you orchids,' he said roughly, releasing her. 'I left them in the kitchen.'

'Why didn't you tell me?' Lynn sent Ginny another one of those exasperated looks and bustled away. 'Eat cake, you lot. I'll put them in water.'

Ginny let the others admire her bracelet then, conscious that Mark was watching her, she busied herself cutting the shortcake Lynn had made, concentrating hard to stop her shaking hands making a mess of the task.

When Lynn returned with the flowers Ginny buried her nose in the blooms, sniffing appreciatively, but although they looked lovely, unlike the flowers Miles had given her there was no scent.

'Where do you want them?' Lynn was helping herself to cake with the others, but she looked around expectantly. 'In here?'

'I'll take them home.' Miles's flowers were so beautiful she didn't need the orchids in her office as well.

Mark was beside her. 'Put them in your bedroom,' he muttered under his breath. 'Donald will be beside himself.'

Ginny stiffened. 'What a good idea,' she said brittlely. 'I'll remember to tell him.'

Mark's regard turned opaque. He opened his mouth but Lynn returned at that moment and, instead of the icy remark Ginny had steeled herself for, he said merely, 'The cake's fantastic, Lynn. Up to your usual standard.'

'Flatterer.' Lynn grinned at him then looked at Ginny again. 'So, what's the birthday girl up to tonight? Dinner on the town with Neil after his lecture or are you going down to London?'

'Just an early night, I think,' Ginny said roughly.

'Really?' Lynn raised her eyebrows teasingly. 'Still like that, is it?' She smiled sentimentally. 'Ah, young love.'

Ginny froze. 'Lynn, you've got it all wrong. Neil and I aren't remotely—'

'Spare us the details,' Mark said abruptly, his tone harsh enough to startle her into biting back the words. He finished his champagne in a single gulp and returned his glass to the table. 'I'm on call and I've work to do. Goodnight, everyone.'

'Goodnight.' Ginny found that she was following him to his office and waiting as he collected his things, hoping, she realised, for some faint lessening in the coldness with which he'd been regarding her. 'Thanks, Mark, really. I love the bracelet.'

Instead of any sign of softening, the look he spared her

was dismissive. 'I bought it months ago,' he said tightly, swinging his briefcase across his desk as he prepared to leave. 'When you liked your Christmas present.'

She stiffened, understanding immediately. 'Relax,' she said sadly. 'I get the message.' She wasn't to think the gift meant anything. 'The shop wouldn't have given you your money back after all this time.'

'Gin, no…' She saw her directness had shocked him and his arm came out to stop her, but she darted past, not wanting him to see the tears that had begun welling again behind her eyes.

'Forget it, Mark. It doesn't matter. See you tomorrow.'

On Friday morning, two days later, she had a brief but busy clinic then rushed away to do her house calls. She arrived back at the surgery with a few minutes to spare before her afternoon session and checked that the kitchen was empty, before making herself coffee.

Lynn joined her, her face creasing into a sympathetic frown as she sat opposite. 'Busy night on call?'

'Fairly.' But it hadn't been her four a.m. call-out to Mr Reeve's heart failure that was responsible for her latest sleepless night—the hour it had taken to treat him and arrange his admission had been a welcome distraction. 'I'm still a little tired.'

The elder woman smiled. 'You're not as young as you used to be,' she teased. 'You'd better start looking after yourself or soon you won't even be able to keep up with Neil.'

Just as she finished speaking the door opened and Mark appeared. He registered the presence of the two of them then hesitated as if undecided whether to stay. Ginny's face froze but Lynn smiled up at him. 'I was teasing Ginny about Neil,' she said lightly. 'He must have kept her up to all hours on her birthday. Poor girl looks exhausted.'

'Really?' His voice was neutral but his gaze was bleak, and Ginny thought she could see some of her own confusion mirrored there. 'As long as her work isn't suffering.'

Lynn laughed, apparently oblivious to the tenseness between the two doctors. 'You can talk,' she chuckled. 'Who is it that asked poor old Mr McGovern yesterday morning how his hysterectomy wound was healing? He thought you'd gone mad!'

'Slip of the tongue.'

'Lack of concentration more like.' Lynn rose, brushing the crumbs from her smart blue uniform. 'You two have been terrible lately but don't think I'm too old to remember what it was like when I was single. I know what you young doctors are like. You're probably as bad as Neil and Ginny, romancing Sarah every night you're not on call. You can't do that and expect to function properly in the morning.'

Ginny hated this. She wasn't up to being involved in a normal conversation yet with Mark, especially with an audience, and she certainly didn't want to hear about anything he did with Sarah. She looked down, willing her attention back to her food although her appetite had vanished. Please go away, she begged silently.

It wasn't Mark who left but Lynn. Even without looking up, she could sense him still in the room.

'I played squash with Bryan Gould last night,' he said formally. She said nothing and he continued, 'He asked me to let you know that your patient, Beryl Scott, is doing well. He thinks you definitely caught that other toe in time to save her foot.'

'Good.' The word sounded croaky and she cleared her throat, before repeating it, then took a careful bite of cheese sandwich.

'If there's nothing else, I'll leave you to it.'

'Fine.' Friday was Mark's half-day and she covered the surgery alone in the afternoon. When it was fine, like today, he played golf with a group of local doctors. If it was too wet for golf, four of them had a permanent booking at some squash courts in Norwich.

There were another few moments of stilted silence and then he swore under his breath and slammed out of the room.

Ginny sagged against the back of the chair. This was awful. More than a week had passed yet she could still barely look at him, let alone talk with him, yet unless they talked they'd never resolve this. At the same time she had no idea what she wanted to say to him. All she knew was that going over and over the event in her head wasn't helping. What she needed was something to distract her. Something hard and physical.

When she finished her afternoon clinic she telephoned Bryan Gould's wife, Jane. She'd met Jane several times at social occasions and had always meant to make more of an effort to get to know her. It was time to try. A secret voice whispered that it would do Mark good to learn he didn't know her as well as he'd assumed—suddenly his blithe assumption he could bet money on her not playing squash seemed smug and irritating.

Jane sounded surprised but pleased to hear from her. 'Ginny, I don't believe you really want to do this. Bryan said he'd given up on winning his fifty pounds.'

Ginny relished the thought of Mark losing the money instead. 'I owe him one. I said I'd give you a call but, I warn you, I haven't played squash since college. Actually I haven't played anything since college. I won't be much of a challenge for you.'

Jane laughed. 'Don't worry. I'm lousy myself but we'll still have fun.' They arranged to meet on Monday evening provided Jane could arrange the court and equipment hire.

As she replaced the receiver their receptionist's head appeared around the door. 'Dr Hutton's here to see Mark,' she said worriedly, 'but he's on the golf course, isn't he?'

Ginny frowned, pushing back her chair to go and speak with him. 'I'm sorry, Donald. Mark's playing golf this afternoon. Is there something I can help you with?'

The grey-haired doctor looked at his watch. 'Not to worry, Virginia. I'm a little early. I came straight from my calls. He's meeting me here after his round.' He looked at her expectantly. 'Any chance of a cup of tea?'

'Of course.' Resisting the impulse to shock him by suggesting he prepare his own, she led him through into the kitchen and threw a teabag into a cup. 'Thank you for my birthday flowers. They're beautiful.'

'Then they complement you perfectly,' he returned smoothly.

Ginny rolled her eyes as she poured the milk. 'How's Mary?'

'Well.'

She passed him his cup, preparing to make an excuse and escape, but he patted the space beside him. 'Sit down, Virginia. We're both so busy we rarely get a chance to chat.'

For the sake of practice harmony Ginny summoned a polite smile and sat stiffly, uncomfortable about the way he shifted closer. 'I saw one of your patients last night, Moira Fields, with a worsening of her asthma. I bumped up her steroids to forty milligrams,' she told him. 'Did you get my note?'

'I did, indeed.' He nodded. 'Thank you.' He straightened his tie and cleared his throat. 'And thank you for your help with Mr Gates last week. You'll be pleased to know he's doing well after his heart attack. He's on the ward now, out of Coronary Care. He'll probably be discharged after the weekend.'

'I'm glad.'

'He had no cardiac history at all. No hypertension and his cholesterol was quite normal and he's never even smoked. He's a widower, you know. Lived alone for the best part of ten years.' He beamed at her. 'When something like that happens out of the blue it reinforces my belief that you should make the best of your life,' he said heartily. '"Seize the day", and all that. Don't you agree?'

'I…suppose so,' Ginny said slowly, wondering where this was leading. When Donald leaned towards her and took her hand in his, she glimpsed a possibility and promptly froze with shock.

'Virginia, my dear,' he said fervently, peering at her intently through faintly misted spectacles, 'I realise you're very young but I hope that doesn't mean an old man like me can't make you happy. I don't believe I've ever told you how extraordinarily beautiful I find you. You've quite the most perfect skin I've ever seen. So pale. I can't help but wonder if it's as soft as it—'

At the very moment his hand touched her cheek there was a noise from the door. Ginny spun around and her wide, startled eyes met Mark's.

'Sorry,' he said icily. 'Shall I come back later?'

'No,' she gasped, finally finding the power to lurch away from Donald and out of the seat. 'No, stay. Discuss your tournament or whatever. I—I was just leaving.'

The older man stood too. 'Virginia…?'

'No, Donald.' She evaded his seeking hand, by swerving fiercely around him, and flinched from Mark's I-told-you-so expression as he leaned against the wall, his arms crossed.

'I have huge respect for you professionally,' she continued, her eyes flickering back to Donald, 'but there can never be anything more to our relationship than work. I'm sorry if I've ever given you any other impression.'

After that she fled to her office, slammed the door and

lowered her head to her hands, not sure whether to laugh or cry but in reality too distraught to do either. 'Oh, God,' she groaned. Yet another thing to worry about.

Then she sat up, paling, wondering if she'd made a mistake in leaving the two men alone. Mark had never concealed his revulsion about the thought of her and Donald together. What if they came to blows?

However, she couldn't hear any raised voices, and after a tense fifteen minutes she heard Donald leave. She sat, rigid, waiting for Mark. Would he want to talk about it? Would he be sympathetic about what had happened or would he be angry? Where Donald was concerned, she was unhappily aware that he had a short tether.

He wasn't long. The corridor was carpeted and his steps were light, but she was so sensitive to him at the moment that even if he'd tiptoed she'd have known he was there. She caught her breath, waiting for the door to open, but— apart from a tiny hesitation, which could easily have been in her imagination—he didn't pause.

Ginny shoved back her chair hurriedly and reached for the door. Surely he wasn't leaving for the weekend, without speaking to her? 'Mark, wait…'

'What?' He'd been about to go out the side door to the car park and had his hand on the handle, but he turned, his face cool and impatient, checking his watch as if he were in a hurry.

She hesitated, regretting leaving her office. 'I… Can we talk?'

His mouth tightened. 'About Donald?'

'About everything.' His expression didn't change and she turned away. 'OK, forget it. There's no point when you're like this.'

She tried to slam her door but Mark moved quickly, jamming his foot in the doorway and forcing it open. 'Forget what?'

She backed towards her desk and then, realising she must look feeble, forced herself to stay still. 'I thought you were in a rush to leave?'

'Stop trying to distract me.' He leaned back and the door clicked shut. 'If you've something to say,' he added wearily, 'I'm listening. Tell me, Ginny.'

But Ginny wasn't sure exactly what she wanted to say at all. All she wanted was for things to get back to normal—for them to talk again and for him never to leave without saying goodbye to her. She looked at him now and she was flustered—it had become a reflex.

Mark moved. He propped himself against her examination couch and regarded her darkly. He slid his hands into the pockets of his golfing pants, which drew the cream cloth taut across his powerful thighs, forcing her to drag her gaze away.

'I'm sorry...about Donald.'

'Sorry?' One eyebrow lifted doubtfully. 'You don't have to apologise to me,' he said coolly. 'How you conduct your...love life is your own business.'

'Donald's nothing to do with my love life,' she protested. 'What are you saying?'

'That you've never exactly discouraged him.'

'You know it's not like that,' she said fiercely, and sank onto her chair, her hands gripping the armrests so hard her knuckles turned white. 'I only try to be nice to him for the sake of our roster. You're twisting everything.'

She saw his hands ball into fists. 'The stupidest thing is that I was worried about you,' he grated. 'I thought something was up when he insisted we meet here. I made sure I was back early but I was wasting my bloody time, wasn't I? All I did was interrupt the big seduction scene.'

Ginny shook her head frantically. 'You don't believe that.'

'Don't I?' Perhaps her words reached him because his

voice quietened, but his regard remained narrow and assessing. 'Let's just say I'm not sure what I believe right now.'

She lowered her head. 'If it's any consolation, I feel the same,' she said quietly, 'but it doesn't make sense to get angry about things. What happened, happened. I can't pretend I understand why it did or why we let ourselves get into this mess but I know we can't go on fighting or ignoring each other for the next six months.'

'Six months?' Mark laughed briefly and harshly. 'You think I could still go to Sarah?'

Ginny's eyes bulged. 'Oh, my God. Mark, you didn't—?'

'It's over.'

'But if you explain—'

'This is about you and me, Ginny. Nothing to do with Sarah.'

She spun her chair to the window, staring at it blindly. 'I don't think the fact that we slept together one time sh—'

'Neither of us slept,' he interjected.

'The fact that we had *sex*,' she said crisply, 'shouldn't change our lives. It was just one act. We're adults. Sometimes these things just happen. We have to deal with this and move on.'

She heard him shift and lifted her head, watching his reflection against the dark trunk of the willow outside. He stood in front of her desk, studying her as she studied him. 'One act,' he echoed cynically. 'Are you trying to tell me you have that sort of sex with Neil all the time?'

Ginny stiffened. 'Neil and I have never had a sexual relationship,' she said tightly. 'But believe what you want. God knows, when it comes to him you always have.'

'I'm sorry.' Abruptly she saw the anger drain from him. 'Gin, I'm sorry. I don't mean to be like this.'

'It's all right.' She turned slowly, suddenly aching to

comfort him, but wariness held her away. 'We're both still confused. We made a mistake, one we can't take back, and we just have to learn to live with it. It'll get easier.'

'It had better.' The eyes that met hers were dark and unreadable, and his grip on her door as he wrenched it open looked vicious. 'All I can say is that it had better.'

# CHAPTER FIVE

ON CALL from Saturday morning, Ginny woke after a night tortured with alarming dreams about Mark, relieved at the thought of not having to spend another weekend alone with her thoughts. Her work would distract her.

However, the weekend began extraordinarily quietly. After the regular Saturday morning clinic she had very little else to do. She had to get up only once during the night to visit a young man, complaining of chest pains—pains which happily turned out to be secondary to too many lagers and a late night spicy curry.

On Sunday morning she had two calls, neither requiring a visit, and in the afternoon she went into the surgery, weary of thinking about Mark and of the guilt and needing something to divert her mind—even if it was only paperwork.

She sighed as she surveyed the mound of forms that needed to be completed. Despite her efforts the previous weekend, much had re-accumulated. She had vaccination and immunisation claim forms, fitting of IUD forms, minor surgery fee forms, health promotion clinic forms, emergency treatment forms, night visit claim forms...all equally boring, all equally time-consuming. She glared at them, frustrated.

She'd entered medicine to treat patients, not fill in forms, but it appeared that, despite employing a part-time practice manager, both she and Mark were still expected to acquire the skills of a secretary and bookkeeper just to keep up with administration.

The expense of hiring Miles full time would be considerable but perhaps it would be worthwhile.

Crossly she tapped at the computer keyboard, needing the names of patients who'd attended her last minor-surgical list. Then she transferred the details to the appropriate form, keeping a copy for their own records. That done, she shuffled through the rest of her pile.

For another hour or so she worked erratically, increasingly exasperated by the mindless tasks. What was the point in doing a medical degree when she had to work as an accountant? Angrily she threw down her pen and shoved her chair away from the desk.

This wasn't going to work, she acknowledged. She knew the reason for her ill temper and it had nothing to do with paperwork. She knew why she couldn't concentrate.

She pushed herself out of the chair and moved over to the window, staring out sightlessly. She'd met Mark on her first day at medical school. It had been an old-fashioned college, with students paired alphabetically as work and study partners so she'd found herself linked with him for most classes and laboratory sessions.

They were the same age although he'd seemed older, relaxed and sure of himself, subdued where she was high-spirited, thoughtful where she was prone to leap too quickly and academically brilliant where she'd had to work hard. Despite those differences they'd become friends immediately.

Her father had died when she was five and her memories of him were mostly from photographs. She'd been brought up by her well-intentioned but emotionally distant mother. In the years up until Ginny had started university, her mother, an assistant editor for a very traditional women's magazine, had rarely dated.

Ginny had been stunned when she returned from a business trip to Australia within a month of Ginny starting medical school to announce that she'd agreed to marry an Australian man she'd only just met. The wedding was to be in less than a month, in Adelaide in South Australia, and she was emigrating.

Mark had only known Ginny a short time yet he'd sensed how lost she'd been feeling and how shy she'd been about meeting her new stepfather and his children. He'd also loaned her the money for the flight—money her normally efficient mother had overlooked she'd need—and had taken two weeks out of his studies to come with her to the wedding. That thoughtfulness and generosity, together with the fun they'd had, had cemented their relationship.

After graduation they'd been offered jobs at the same hospital and those jobs had led to the same GP training rotation. Later they'd gone into practice together.

It had all been so easy. She'd been convinced that their relationship was secure, which made it so much more disturbing that within one night they'd swung from platonic friendship to a fleeting desire so violent that they'd risked that friendship for something as transient as sexual satisfaction.

No, 'fleeting' was the wrong word, she reflected grimly, resting her forehead against the cool glass of the window. At least it was proving so in her case as images of Mark filled practically every moment of her day, awake and asleep.

The sound of the side door being unlocked made her breath catch and she spun, waiting. All the permanent staff had keys but Mark was the only person likely to be here on a Sunday.

Her door was open and he didn't walk past but merely stopped in the doorway, his calm appraisal suggesting he'd been expecting to find her here.

He looked tired, she realised. Probably as tired as she did. 'Gin, I wanted to say sorry again,' he said quietly. 'On

Friday I was angry with you and with Donald, but mostly with myself. I said a lot of things I know aren't true.'

She swallowed. 'I'm sorry too,' she admitted hesitantly.

He walked into the office and leaned heavily against her desk. 'I know you've never encouraged Donald.'

She nibbled on her lower lip. 'Mark, I could talk to Sarah. I could make her understand—'

He held up his hand. 'That wouldn't help,' he said flatly, and the cold finality in his tone convinced her. 'We've talked. It's over. I'm not going to Scotland.'

'Oh.' She dropped her eyes. 'I'm…sorry it didn't work out.' She took a deep breath. 'I'm sorry that what happened destroyed things. But I am glad you're staying.'

'It's not going to be easy.' She felt his gaze probing the curtain of her hair. 'For either of us.'

She lifted her face again. 'I want it to go back to the way it was before.' Then she tensed, alarmed by his watchful silence. 'Can it?'

Mark's darkly watchful eyes probed hers. 'Are you sure that's what you want?'

'I don't want an affair,' she said hoarsely, recoiling faintly from his regard. 'Not with you.' She knew that she'd never be sophisticated enough to be able to work with him calmly as if it had never happened once it was over. 'I couldn't.' Her physical awareness of him would fade in time, and now she craved their friendship. 'Just friends. Like before. Please, Mark.'

For a few moments their eyes held. Hers, she knew, were soft and pleading, his more guarded, frustrated possibly, but finally he said heavily, 'We can try.'

She managed a weak smile and held up her hand. 'OK?'

'OK.' Mark took her hand, held it very briefly in his warm grip, then released her.

Ginny smiled shyly, still unsure. 'Coffee to celebrate?'

'I'll get it.' Idly he picked one of the forms off the top

of her 'to do' pile, his mouth curling as he dumped it back again. 'And then I'll leave you to this rubbish.' He strode to the door.

While he was out of the room her bleeper shrilled. She dialled her service, wrote down the telephone number of the patient who'd called her and then phoned her.

When she hung up Mark was standing in the doorway, holding their drinks. 'Trouble?'

She nodded. Nellie Jarvis, the elderly woman who was terminally ill with advanced cancer, was one of his patients. 'It was one of Mrs Jarvis's daughters. Nellie's been unwell all weekend and now she's started vomiting.' She stood. 'Sorry about the coffee. I'd better go and see her straight away.'

He rested the cups on her desk. 'I'll come with you.'

'No!' His raised eyebrows flustered her into an explanation. 'It's your day off, Mark. I'm quite capable of looking after the patients.'

'I'm aware of that,' he said gently, 'and normally I wouldn't dream of interfering, but I know Nellie much better than you. If she needs hospitalising you'll have a hell of a job convincing her. Two of us together will have a better chance.'

Ginny sighed but his words made sense. 'OK, thanks.'

They took Mark's car and within ten minutes he was parking outside their patient's home. One of a chain of terraced flats in a rather dingy estate, its flower-filled front garden and colourful window-boxes made it stand out from the rest. Ginny inhaled the sweet fragrances appreciatively as they walked up the path.

Clearly someone had been watching for their arrival because the door opened before she had a chance to knock. 'Oh, Doctors, thank goodness you've arrived.' Nellie's eldest daughter, Sylvia, looked drawn with worry. 'She didn't want me to call you. I had to insist.'

'You did the right thing,' Ginny assured her, concerned with the way Sylvia was wringing her hands. She was prone to angina, secondary to her ischaemic heart disease, and fretting like this wasn't good for her. 'Is she upstairs?'

'That's right.' Sylvia led the way. 'She was all right last week but she's been ill since Friday night. The nurse came yesterday but Mum didn't tell her anything. Then today she's been sick again and again.'

'Any pain?' asked Mark.

Sylvia shook her head. 'I don't think so. Not that she says, but you know how she is.'

'I know.' Mark touched her arm as they paused outside Nellie's room. 'We won't be long. Make us all a pot of tea, hmm?'

Ginny was shocked by her first sight of Nellie. Lying frail and tired in the big bed, her skin matched the hue of the huge vase of scented pale freesias on the dresser at her side. Although Mark had kept Ginny up to date on her illness and she knew Nellie was dying, it had been at least six months since she'd last seen the elderly lady. She'd never been a big woman but now she was tiny.

'Oh, they shouldn't have bothered you, Doctors.' Despite being so unwell, there was a determined twinkle in her eyes as she surveyed the pair of them. 'I'm not dead yet and I'm certainly not going to let you take me away from here!'

Ginny remained standing while Mark took over, crouching by the side of the bed and drawing the covers down with gentle hands. 'What's been happening, Nellie?'

'It's this,' she said weakly, jabbing at the little syringe in a leather holder which delivered pain relief through a needle directly under the skin of her abdomen. 'I'm sure of it. I should never have let that nurse talk me into it on Friday. I've never felt so sick in all my life. Those daughters of mine don't believe it. They say that it's supposed to stop the sickness.'

Mark frowned. 'There's something in it that's supposed to stop nausea,' he admitted, 'but perhaps it doesn't work for you. Have you been in pain?'

She shook her head. 'Not so bad. It's worked for that.'

'Tummy working?'

'Not as well as usual but I'm not blocked up. I'm thirsty, though. Can't keep anything down.'

'Waterworks all right?'

Nellie nodded.

Ginny looked on while Mark examined Nellie carefully. He checked her pulse and skin turgor for signs of dehydration then probed her abdomen gently and listened for bowel sounds with the stethoscope Ginny handed him. She helped Nellie sit up so that he could listen to the back of her chest and then, while she assisted her back on the pillows, he lifted the blankets back and checked her legs and ankles.

'Nellie,' he said gently, 'I'm going to stop this pump tonight and give you an injection for pain and to take away the sickness.'

Ginny passed him a cotton swab from her case and he quickly pulled out the subcutaneous needle from Nellie's abdomen, wiping the site clean. He dropped the needle into a small yellow sharps container she carried for the purpose and gave her the syringe to drop into her rubbish bag.

Nellie watched his movements, sighing as he left the leather case sitting beside the flowers on her dresser. 'You mean you're not going to try and persuade me to go back to that awful hospital?'

'Only if you promise me you'll drink everything Sylvia puts in front of you. You're dehydrated.'

'Ah, you're a good lad.' She gave him a sweet smile, her relief obvious. 'I'll be all right now this is gone.' She eyed the empty case with suspicion.

'If the medicine I bring tomorrow isn't good enough, you might need another one,' he warned, 'but next time I'll use something stronger for the sickness. There's no need for you to suffer.'

She nodded. 'I trust you.' Her eyes drifted closed. 'I feel better already.'

Ginny searched through the small supply of ampoules she carried with her. 'Droperidol?'

'That'll do.' He unwrapped a small syringe and a needle while she snapped the top off the glass container and then he drew it up, together with half an ampoule of diamorphine. He swabbed the outside of his patient's thigh with a sterile alcohol swab. 'Nellie, sharp prick now.'

She didn't even wince as he injected the drugs. Quietly Ginny extracted several sachets of rehydration solution, passing them to Mark in exchange for the empty needle and syringe. Then she packed everything away and snapped the bag locks closed.

Sylvia was waiting for them downstairs. Over tea, Mark explained that her mother's nausea was caused by the opiate she was now receiving for pain relief. He told her that he'd given Nellie something to cover the pain and sickness for a few hours and that he'd come back that evening to give her more. He gave her the rehydration solutions, showing her the instructions for making up the solution. 'She needs at least two of these tonight. More if she can manage it.'

Sylvia nodded, her relief obvious. 'What if she's sick again before you come back?'

'Call me. You've got my direct number so don't go through the service. If the pain relief wears off in the meantime let me know as well.'

'That's a relief,' he said, as they walked back out towards the car. 'I was worried she might have obstructed. I was almost certain she'd refuse to go to hospital. If she'd refused bypass surgery we'd have had a hell of a job controlling her pain.'

'You're very fond of her,' she said, nodding her thanks as he opened her door.

He nodded. 'She's a strong lady. She started fading before Christmas but she's told me she's determined not to die until the end of summer. She's always been a keen gardener and she's vowed to see her roses through one more season.' He looked back towards the house. 'Now every time I look at her I think she's near death but then she opens those sparkling eyes and starts talking and I realise it's only her body that's giving up. Her spirit is as bright as ever.'

Ginny swallowed as he started the car. She knew exactly what he meant. 'I'm glad you came, Mark. I don't think I could have given her quite the lift you did.'

He shrugged. 'You're a fine doctor, Ginny.'

Ginny was confident about her medical skills, but Mark had a special ability to inspire and comfort his patients which she envied. Over the years she'd realised that it was intrinsic to his nature, not something taught in medical school.

He dropped her back at the surgery but shook his head at her offer of a fresh coffee, merely waving before he drove off. Inwardly, Ginny was relieved. They'd declared a truce but the tension hadn't gone, nor had the awareness of how much had changed. It might be a long time before either of them would relax again.

In the middle of Monday afternoon's clinic Jane rang to confirm their squash date for that evening. Ginny was too busy to do anything but note down the time—which was fortunate, she decided later. If she'd had more time to think she'd probably have tried to get out of the arrangement.

It was with more than mild apprehension that she eyed the racquet the attendant handed her that evening. Ginny was quite happy to admit that her strengths were academic, not physical, and organised sport bored her silly. It had been years since she'd participated in any exercise more energetic than the occasional country rambles Mark forced upon her. 'Prepare to be humiliated,' she mumbled dryly, making a token effort to copy Jane's fluid series of stretches.

'Ready?' Her companion's smile was enthusiastic as she completed her warm-up.

Ginny grimaced but didn't say anything before she followed her unhappily onto the court, cursing the impulse to get the better of Mark which had led her into this.

Forty minutes later she wasn't any happier. Tired, hot, breathless and sweaty, yes. But definitely not happy.

'Good match.'

She shot her opponent a sidelong glance as they walked out of the court. 'You must be joking!' she managed between pants. 'I didn't win a single game.'

Jane laughed, bending to pick up a towel and wipe her face. 'No, really. You were OK. I thought you hadn't played for years?'

'Since college,' Ginny acknowledged. She rested her racquet on the ground and leaned against the wall of the corridor, waiting for her breathing to slow. 'Wasn't it obvious?' she heaved. 'I played terribly.'

'Nonsense.' Jane gave her a pat on the shoulder. 'A few more sessions and you'll be great.'

'Don't hold your breath.' She lifted her head at the sound of approaching voices then groaned. A grinning Bryan and a stunned-looking Mark, both in sports gear, were apparently just about to take over their court.

'Hi, girls!' chirped Bryan, his wink at Jane and his obvious delight making it clear this wasn't a coincidence. He slapped Mark across the back. 'That's fifty pounds you owe me, partner.'

Ginny shifted uncomfortably. Mark was disturbingly attractive in his brief shorts and white sports shirt, and it continued to bother her that she kept noticing him in that way. 'We've just finished,' she said lamely, sure that was perfectly obvious given the no doubt puce colour of her face. 'But I wouldn't make any bets on me playing again,' she added to Bryan, her gaze flicking nervously away from Mark. 'Ever.'

Bryan's grin widened. 'You never know,' he countered. 'Exercise is addictive.'

Wanting to escape as quickly as possible, she merely made a noncommittal sound before she retrieved her racquet. 'Have a good game,' she said, standing aside so they could open the door to the court.

Mark let Bryan precede him, pausing beside her as his opponent took a few practice swipes through the air. 'Well done,' he said coolly.

Their eyes met and beneath his shrewd gaze Ginny flushed. 'I—I wasn't just trying to make you lose your money,' she stammered. 'I virtually promised Bryan a few weeks ago when he saw Beryl Scott for me.'

'I wasn't implying anything,' Mark countered quietly. 'I meant it. Well done. I know how much you hate this sort of thing. I'm glad you decided to play. Let me know if you want another game.'

'Oh.' She hardly knew where to look. 'Thank you.'

For a few seconds they just stood there, then the sound of Bryan's ball hitting the metal grid on the court seemed to startle Mark and he turned away abruptly and slammed the door behind him.

Ginny's legs trembled as she followed Jane along the corridor towards the showers, and grimly she acknowledged that it wasn't just the unaccustomed exercise which was responsible.

Next morning Mark caught her in the corridor as she was hobbling towards the side door, about to leave for her house calls. 'Ginny, Lynn's away this afternoon—parents' day or something at Lisa's school. I've a medical student with me today so do you want his help this afternoon?'

'Yes, please,' she said huskily, her mouth suddenly uncomfortably dry. In his dark suit Mark was nowhere near as disturbingly informal as he'd been in his squash clothes but still his impact on her pulse was unmistakable and she squirmed inside uncomfortably. If they were to work effectively she had to try harder to overcome this.

'How many on the list?'

List? Ginny frowned vaguely, but when his eyes narrowed her thoughts cleared abruptly. He meant her minor surgical list, the one scheduled for this afternoon—the one his medical student was going to help her with. 'S-six or seven, I think,' she said quickly, 'so I'd appreciate a hand. Thanks. That's very thoughtful.'

He leaned against the wall, his eyes lazily curious. 'Any problems from the squash last night? Stiff yet?'

She flushed, wondering if he'd seen how she'd been walking. 'I could hardly get out of bed this morning,' she admitted breathlessly, relieved that, despite her jerking pulse, she was managing to hold a normal conversation. 'And my back...' she rubbed the particularly sore area between her shoulders, deciding it wouldn't be a good idea to ask him for one of his magic massages '...has definitely seen better days.'

'It'll be worse tomorrow,' he said with mock sympathy.

He grinned at her disgusted expression and turned away, and Ginny stared after him, puzzled by why it felt as if the sun had suddenly come out. It took her a few seconds to realise it was because it seemed like the first time he'd smiled at her in ages.

Before Lynn left that afternoon she'd clearly taken the time to set up the small but well-equipped treatment room that doubled as a theatre in preparation for the clinic, for when Ginny arrived there was a neat array of labelled packages, containing the equipment she required for each procedure.

Mark's student, Jason, was a cheerful, capable helper who already had her laughing with his anecdotes by the time their first patient arrived.

While he helped her with the first case—removal of a rather large lipoma, or fatty swelling, from her patient's back—he kept them both entertained, by discussing the way they'd been taught to suture by one of their surgical tutors.

'We weren't allowed near a model, let alone a patient, until we could sew up an empty banana skin perfectly,' he chirped. 'I took weeks to get it right. I spent hours sewing bananas. Half my grant was going to support my habit. I was eating so many bananas I started to smell like one.'

After she'd finished, still laughing, Ginny disposed of the used instruments while they waited for the next case.

'You're incredibly neat,' said Jason. 'That wound was perfect. Have you done a lot of surgery?'

She shrugged. 'The usual six months as a house surgeon and a casualty job which included a lot of minor ops. Then a couple of years ago both Mark and I did a one-week intensive course run by Bryan Gould, one of the local surgeons.'

'A course for GPs?'

She nodded. 'That sort of training is important. In hospitals as junior doctors we tend to tackle most things, knowing back-up's always available, but GPs need to bear in mind their limitations. Courses like the one we did point out what they should be. We just do cysts and minor lesions here. Anything more complicated we refer to the specialists.'

They worked steadily through the list and for the rest of the cases, with the permission of her patients, Ginny let

Jason suture the wounds while she supervised. Clearly the banana training had paid off because he was a careful, precise worker, far more confident than she'd been at his stage.

Just before five, while Ginny laid out a new sterile instrument tray, he welcomed their seventh and last patient into the room, a pale, nervous-looking young man with a small cyst on his forehead. 'Get yourself up here, then. That's it. Lie back.'

She scrubbed her hands and pulled on sterile gloves, listening to Jason argue good-naturedly with the patient about the abilities—or, rather, lack of them—of the local football team. While they bickered she cleaned the area and draped his forehead with paper guards. 'Bit of a sting now,' she warned, as she injected lignocaine, containing a small amount of adrenaline, beneath the skin to numb the region and minimise any bleeding.

While the two of them discussed penalties and yellow cards she made a smooth elliptical incision, gently freed the cyst with her forceps and carefully extracted the pea-like swelling intact. Within a few minutes Jason had scrubbed and was stitching the wound neatly closed.

When he'd finished, Ginny covered the area with a small dressing, and their patient sat up, probing the plaster experimentally. 'I hardly felt a thing.'

'That was the idea,' said Ginny dryly, smiling her thanks to Jason. In her experience young men were the most nervous of all when it came to this sort of thing, but Jason's cheerful banter had kept him distracted. 'Come back on Monday and we'll take your stitches out.'

'Great. Thanks.' He sauntered jauntily out of the room.

Ginny smiled again as she dumped the last of the disposable instruments into the sharps disposal unit. 'Well done. Are you interested in surgery as a career?'

'Maybe now.' He was grinning as he labelled the last specimen for her so that it was ready to go to the laboratory.

'But I still get this funny surprised feeling when I lift up the skin and there isn't any yellow banana flesh underneath.'

She was still laughing as she followed him out of the theatre. Mark was in the corridor, looking over the appointment book with one of the receptionists, and when he heard Jason and Ginny laughing his head came up and he glared at her.

Ginny sobered. Whatever it was she'd done, she was feeling too fragile to face an argument, especially after they'd been getting on relatively well again. After thanking Jason for his help, she retreated to her office and shut the door firmly behind her. She hurried as she threw a couple of journals she wanted to read into a bag and collected her coat, but the receptionist put a call through to her from a drug-company rep, wanting to make an appointment to see her, and when she hung up she could feel Mark's eyes on her. When she swung around he was standing there.

'He's a little young, isn't he, Ginny? Even for you?'

She paled. 'What are you talking about?'

'Take a wild guess.'

'Don't be ridiculous.' She stared at him in despair. 'Stop it, Mark. Neither of us wants an argument.'

'Oh, I don't know,' he said roughly. 'An argument's exactly what I need right now.'

'It's obviously what you're looking for.' She picked up her bag, her mouth tight.

'Exactly how many men do you need?' he snapped. 'Does it give you a kick to see them all lusting after you? He's still a bloody student, for God's sake!'

'Don't be disgusting.' She marched for the door but he blocked it. 'I want to leave,' she said stiffly. 'You're in my way.'

'You're not leaving yet,' he grated. 'Jason's in

Reception. Waiting for you. He wants to ask your advice on his career—advice that, apparently, I can't give him.'

She took a deep breath. 'He's a medical student, Mark. Nothing else. I asked him about his career plans. You've no right to say these things to me.' She lifted her head again, meeting the scorn in his glare with brittle calm. 'Now, please, get out of my way.'

He didn't budge. He slid his hands into the pockets of his dark trousers, his gaze coldly assessing. 'Nice try,' he said acidly. 'I might even have believed you if I hadn't seen you myself, flashing your eyes at him, and if I hadn't had to listen to the sound of you giggling like a schoolgirl on her first date all afternoon.'

'He was telling jokes,' she said stiffly.

'Did he excite you?'

'No!' She recoiled, shocked. 'This is all in your imagination. I don't understand any of this.'

'Try frustration.'

Ginny flushed a hot red. She reeled away from him, heading for the other door that opened into the back corridor, but he was quick and he caught her arm before she was halfway across the room.

'Oh, no, you don't.' He lifted her onto her chair then propped himself against her desk and pulled the chair towards him, his arms on either side, trapping her. 'Stop acting like the maidenly aunt I know you're not.'

She pushed herself as far back in the chair as she could. 'I never started any of this,' she said faintly. 'It was you.'

'You came to me,' he grated. 'You knew what I wanted that night but you didn't stay away. Why, Ginny, why? Tell me! If it wasn't for sex, why did you come? What did you want from me?'

She could explain why she'd gone to his house but she wasn't sure he'd believe her. She even wondered if she believed it herself.

She'd told herself at the time that it was so she could help him resolve his confusion about their relationship and his problems with Sarah, but had there been more to it than that?

Lately, her awareness of him had made her look harder at her motivation and the memory that she spent at least half that evening at Sarah's speculating about Mark's love-making skills had shaken her. Was it possible that she'd been as jealous of Sarah that night as the other woman had been of her? Was it possible that she'd subconsciously *planned* what had happened? Was that why she'd not made any attempt to resist him?

'I'm not some sort of *femme fatale*,' she protested.

'Neil, me, Donald.' His mouth twisted. '*"Femme fatale"* is a little tame, isn't it?'

'Please, Mark.' She sagged in her chair, her eyes closing, weary of trying to work everything out, too weary to fight him. 'Don't say these things. You know none of it's true.'

'Oh, Gin, don't cry.' All at once he was there, lifting her from her chair, his arms mercifully gentle around her. 'I'm sorry. Of course I do. I just…find myself reacting to things lately. I seem to spend half my days apologising to you.' His voice was husky against her ears. 'Forgive me.'

'Yes.' Her chest lifted in a sob, but he was warm and comforting and she was content to be surrounded by him. 'I'm sorry for everything, too. I never… I miss you so much.'

'Shh,' he soothed. 'I'm here. I'm always here.' His fingers under her chin tilted her head and she blinked at him, knowing even before his head moved what was going to happen.

His kiss was soft and coaxing and his gentleness over-whelmed her. Unresisting, she let him taste her. It went on and on and it was as if she were dissolving. When he lifted his head again she could barely think.

'Not like this, Gin.' His voice was deep and rasping. 'Not again. We have to agree on taking this one way or the other.' He was forcing her back to reality despite her efforts to forget it. 'We can't just let it happen again.'

His touch was appallingly, gnawingly tempting and unconsciously she swayed towards him. 'If we do, what happens when it's over?' she whispered. 'I'll find it so hard to work together but I don't want our partnership to end. Will you help me or will you just want me to go away? Will everything change? Will we ever be able to be friends again?'

'I don't know.' While she stayed there, numb, throbbing from his kiss, he drew back, his look long and darkly assessing. 'I can't make any promises, Ginny. Not yet. It's too soon.'

Her hands clutched at the desk and she longed for him to make it easy for her, longed for him to reassure her—pretend, if he had to, even though he never pretended. But he didn't move and finally she found a voice, a dull, husky voice. 'It's just a physical thing. It's not worth sacrificing everything else.'

'Your decision, Ginny.' His expression was unreadable, but his movements as he went to the door were taut and controlled. 'You know it always was.'

# CHAPTER SIX

MONDAY morning, two months later, Ginny stood in the kitchen, gulping her coffee so she'd be finished before patients started to arrive for her clinic. She watched Mark warily though her lashes.

Although he was flicking through a journal, apparently at ease, a disagreement, usually—no not *usually*, she corrected herself, but *always*—over something trivial had become part of their morning ritual these last weeks. Today, though, tired of the bickering, she'd steeled herself neither to provoke nor respond.

So far all had been civil. Had Mark made the same sort of vow himself? She lifted her eyes briefly to the ceiling. The irony of that, when lately they hadn't even been able to agree on where in the waiting-room to hang their latest health-promotion posters, didn't bear thinking about.

'Ginny?' Lynn's head appeared around the door. 'Mary Turnball's here.'

Ginny saw Mark's head come up sharply but she kept her eyes averted. 'Thanks. I'll be right along.' She swallowed the rest of her coffee and moved to the sink to rinse her cup.

Quietly, Mark said, 'Seen Donald lately?'

Ginny stiffened. Mary was Donald's daughter so it wasn't unreasonable of him to raise the topic of their fellow GP, but he was someone they'd both avoided discussing. 'The meeting last week, that's all.'

Mark's eyes narrowed. 'I noticed he couldn't keep his eyes off you.' The words came out jerkily, as if he was trying to hold them back but couldn't manage it.

'Don't be ridiculous.' Her nails curled into her palms. 'You heard me tell him how I felt that day he came here.'

'Telling men "no" doesn't always help,' he grated, standing.

'Well, there's not much more I can do,' she snapped. She brushed past him as she headed for the door, flinching from his touch. Her body's awareness of him hadn't diminished a fraction. Simple things—like passing cups of coffee or notes, walking past him—were fraught with clumsiness. She was still totally aware of him and totally self-conscious, and she hated it.

Knowing her face must still show signs of strain, she summoned a smile as she went to greet her patient. 'Mary, hi!' She smiled at the young baby Mary carried across her front in a colourful sling. Although she approved of the method, she wondered what Mary's father thought of it. She suspected he was probably an ardent supporter of the traditional, cumbersome pram. 'How's Phoebe?'

'She's fine.' Mary slumped into the chair beside Ginny's desk. 'No problems since the six-week check Dr Reynolds did. She's lovely. Left alone, she'll even sleep right through.' She bent to nuzzle the child's dark hair, then lifted her head again. 'No, it's me,' she said. 'I think I might be pregnant again.'

Ginny's eyebrows lifted. 'Really? Already?'

Mary blushed. 'I'm afraid we didn't wait very long after the birth,' she admitted. 'And now I'm not sure. Because I'm breast-feeding I didn't think it was possible, but I've got all the symptoms.'

'It *is* possible,' Ginny conceded. 'Breast-feeding doesn't always give the total protection most people assume but, really, Mary, it's very early. Not that that's bad,' she added hurriedly, seeing the girl's face fall, 'as long as you're happy.'

'If it's true, I'm thrilled.' She gazed down at her sleeping baby. 'Giles and I both want a big family and the sooner the better, as far as I'm concerned.'

'Tell me about your symptoms.'

'Well, still no period, although I know that can be quite normal, of course. I'm constantly up and down to the bathroom and my breasts are incredibly sensitive, much more than they were a week ago, even though I've been breast-feeding the whole time. I felt a bit queasy this morning, but besides that, I just feel, well…pregnant.' She shrugged. 'You know what I mean.'

Ginny nodded, dismissing the vaguely uneasy feeling Mary's words had evoked. Mary's symptoms were normal ones of pregnancy and there was nothing worrying about them.

She directed Mary to the examination couch and took the baby to allow her to undress. She pulled the curtain around to give her some privacy.

She lifted Phoebe, smiled into her healthily plump face and cuddled her against her breast. 'You're beautiful,' she cooed, surprised that the baby hadn't yet started to cry—as they invariably did when she held them. 'Yes, you are, you're beautiful.' Then she looked up, blinking, when Mark appeared at her door.

'I need those forms.' He barely looked at her. 'Miles is going to submit our claims this afternoon.'

'On my desk.' She shifted the baby and pointed to where she'd meant, but Phoebe didn't like being moved. Her blue eyes snapped open, her little face crumpled and, ignoring Ginny's attempt to shush her, she let out a long wail.

'Give her to me.' Mark took the crying baby, and to Ginny's irritation Phoebe quietened instantly. 'Good girl,' he told her, his brown eyes coolly triumphant as he let them meet Ginny's. 'You know who's boss, don't you?'

'Careful, that nappy's wet,' Ginny rasped, the sight of him cradling the tiny baby making her throat lock inexplicably. 'And since you've nothing else to do but look for paperwork you can look after her for me,' she added, seizing the opportunity to return to Mary.

After she'd finished her examination she sent Mary to the bathroom to collect a specimen and, as Lynn was free, asked her to do a pregnancy test. They no longer sent the samples to the laboratory because the test kits they used at the practice were just as accurate and meant an instant result for her patients.

'It's impossible to be sure from the size of your uterus,' she explained to Mary as she took her through into Mark's office to collect her baby. 'Any bulkiness might still be due to Phoebe, anyway.'

She watched Mark pass the contented baby across but, although Ginny sensed his eyes on her, she avoided his gaze, merely muttering her thanks as they left the room.

Five minutes later Lynn popped her head around the door and gave Ginny a thumbs-up gesture.

Ginny smiled at Mary. 'Congratulations. You *are* pregnant.'

Mary whooped her delight. 'Wonderful,' she cried, cuddling her baby closely, her face lit with a wide smile. 'I can't wait to tell Giles.'

'You must take care of yourself, Mary.' Ginny gently warned her about the possibility of miscarriage so early in her pregnancy, especially considering how recently she'd delivered. 'But, all going well and assuming you ovulated six weeks after the delivery, Phoebe will have a baby brother or sister around...' she checked the disc she kept on her desk '...early February probably. We'll have to wait for a scan to be certain.'

'I can't wait.' Mary fitted Phoebe back into the sling across her chest. 'When should I see you again?'

'In about four weeks—earlier if you're worried about anything.' Ginny watched her go, puzzled by her lingering unease. Was it that she regretted warning Mary about the risk of miscarriage? But she'd decided long ago it was important that women were aware of how high the risk was in very early pregnancy and there was no reason for her to avoid the subject with Mary.

She tried to shrug the odd feeling aside but it lingered there throughout the morning, something worried and brooding at the back of her mind.

After seeing her last patient, she collected her lunch from her bag and carried it into the kitchen. Mark was already there, browsing through another journal. He glanced up when she unwrapped her cold toast sandwich. 'That looks revolting, even for you,' he said flatly. 'I'm going out to buy fresh rolls if you can wait.'

Ginny shook her head. 'This'll be fine. It was supposed to be breakfast,' she said stiffly, 'but I wasn't hungry enough.' Wasn't hungry? No, that wasn't quite true. She'd felt a bit sick.

Nauseated even. She'd put the feeling down to the creaminess of the sauce she'd had on her pasta the night before, but now she felt the colour drain from her face. It wasn't the first morning she'd felt unwell lately and it couldn't all be related to food. And her breasts had been sore. No wonder Mary's symptoms had jolted her.

Numbly she looked at Mark, at the very moment he looked up from his reading. His brows drew together. 'What's wrong?' he demanded. 'What's happened? Are you sick?'

Her mouth opened but no words came out.

'Ginny?' There was abrupt concern now in his expression. He dropped the articles he'd been reading and stood to confront her. 'What's going on?'

'I—it's Monday,' she stammered. 'I have to go.'

'You're entitled to your half day.'

'Yes.'

'But I thought you were doing paperwork.'

'No!' But the word sprang out louder than it should have—much louder, awkwardly loud—and his eyes narrowed, suspiciously, she decided, and that made her rush on. 'I've changed my mind. I'll do it tomorrow. I need... I have to go.' She dumped her uneaten lunch in the bin. 'Mark, you...' But she didn't remember what she'd been meaning to say. Wordlessly, she jerked open the door.

'Ginny!'

Mark's command made her freeze. She took a deep breath then turned back. 'What?'

'You're not well. I'll drive you home.'

'No! No, thank you.' She couldn't look at him. 'I'm...fine,' she insisted, pulling the door shut.

She stumbled to her office and flicked frantically through the calendar on her desk, searching the dates. She'd always been irregular—in the past more than two months had often passed without her having a period and she'd never worried about it—but, then, she'd never had unprotected sex before.

She took a kit from the surgery's drug cabinet, drove straight home and tested herself.

An hour later, obeying impulses she didn't understand but knowing she had to get away from the village, she found herself on a train to London's Liverpool Street station. Dragged with the bustle of busy passengers to the Underground entrance, she followed the mob and let herself be swept off again at Oxford Circus.

It was a warm, sticky day, and after a few hours, wandering through the crowds along Oxford Street, she sought refuge in an air-conditioned department store. Her feet found their way to the baby department.

There was so much she didn't know, she realised, bewildered by the displays. She needed so much. Clothes, toys, nappies, carriers, a cot, a pram, blankets, towels, soap and more, so much more. And what about maternity clothes? Didn't she need dresses and special bras and things?

'Next floor,' said the assistant.

So Ginny took the escalator and spent more time looking at clothes, holding them against her to assess the fit. Only when she caught one of the assistants looking at her strangely did her gaze drift to her stomach, and she realised that it was still flat and she didn't need to buy anything yet.

Feeling foolish, she clipped the dress back onto the hanger and fled.

The Underground was steamy and crowded with rush-hour commuters and tourists, and she spent the journey to Liverpool Street jammed against the door to the adjacent carriage. Before the first stop she was feeling light-headed and sweaty. Angry with herself for not having eaten all day, she spent the rest of the journey hanging grimly onto the edge of the door, squeezing the muscles in her calves and concentrating on keeping her breathing deep and regular.

At the British Rail station she just had time to buy sandwiches before she had to hurry for her train. Soon after the train pulled out she ripped off the plastic cover, took a bite and then froze, realising what she'd chosen. Fresh Brie and avocado. Her favourite. But forbidden.

As discreetly as she could, she spat the food into a paper napkin, but the disapproving sniff from the elderly woman opposite suggested that her gesture had not gone unnoticed. Ginny said, 'Sorry. I forgot I'm not supposed to be eating soft cheeses. I'm going to have a baby.'

The woman's expression softened a fraction and the man beside her leaned forward and patted Ginny's hand. 'Congratulations,' he said kindly. 'You must be very pleased.'

'I am.' Her voice sounded husky, and she spoke again, stronger now, 'I am, thank you.' Then she leaned back and her eyes closed and she smiled, and for the first time all day she gave in to the rush of intense, undiluted joy her discovery had kindled. This wasn't going to be easy—nothing was ever going to be easy again—but there was a little life inside her and it felt glorious.

Although still broad daylight, it was after eight when she parked outside her flat. The bottom lock on her door was open and for a few seconds she hesitated. Despite the village's smallness it was, sadly, not immune to burglary and vandalism, and although she'd been feeling rather dazed when she'd left that afternoon she was surprised she'd forgotten to lock the door properly. That sort of thing was usually automatic.

Before she had a chance to insert her key in the top lock the door was wrenched open from inside and Mark glared at her, his face dark. 'Where the hell have you been?'

Ginny blinked. 'How…?'

'Your spares.' He dangled a set of keys.

'But—'

'But nothing.' He took her arm and tugged her inside, gentle despite his obvious impatience, letting the door slam behind them. His arm slid to her back, propelling her ahead of him up the stairs. 'Where were you?'

Ginny swallowed. 'London. Sh-shopping,' she stammered nervously. 'Window-shopping,' she added, when his doubtful eyes dropped to her empty hands.

'I thought you were ill.'

'No…'

'You hate shopping.'

Ginny shook her head vaguely. 'Mark, give me back those keys. You can't just barge in—'

'You didn't answer your phone.' There was no sign of the keys now and he made no mention of them. 'I thought you were sick.'

'I'm not.' She was too tired to cope with him. She felt hot and grubby and light-headed and she needed food. Food would give her strength and the baby nourishment. 'Thanks for being worried,' she said thinly, 'but you can see I'm fine. Please leave the keys.'

But he followed her. He walked into the kitchen just as she was biting into a banana, the only thing she could find that was immediately edible. 'I want to know where you were,' he said, more softly now. 'I deserve that at least.'

She finished her mouthful, watching him warily. The baby would be his too, but right now all she was aware of was a fierce possessiveness. She wanted to keep the knowledge to herself for a little longer. She needed plans, firm, sensible plans. Everything had to be sorted out before she could deal with his reaction. 'London. I don't understand why you were so worried.'

His eyes slid away from hers, focusing on the banana she continued to chew. 'I tried to call Neil but he's at a seminar or something and I couldn't get hold of him.' Her puzzlement must have been obvious because he continued, 'Lynn said you had a call before lunch this morning—before you got ill. I thought it might have been Neil. I thought he might have said something to you.'

She frowned, discarding the peel she clutched before reaching for another banana. 'The call was just a rep,' she said vaguely. 'But what would Neil have said to make you worried?'

'You really don't know?' He pushed his fingers through his hair, gave her a frustrated look, then finally said, 'I shouldn't be the one telling you this.'

She leaned back against the bench as she chewed, feeling slightly more solid now she had some food inside her. 'What?'

'Neil's seeing another woman. I saw them. Saturday. He had his arm around her. Ginny, I'm sorry.'

She blinked. Neil had his arm around another woman? That was wonderful news. And Mark had seen them on

Saturday. She frowned. Where had he been? And who with? Sarah? 'Who was she—the woman with Neil?'

'I don't know.' He ran his hands through his hair, ruffling it again, and Ginny put her free hand behind her back to stop herself smoothing it.

'I still don't understand why you were so worried,' she said huskily, and then she read his doubt, his concern, and her face stilled. 'You thought I might have done something stupid?' she demanded, aghast.

'You seemed very attached.'

'Not in that way.'

'He's the only man you've ever dated more than a few weeks.'

'But that doesn't mean...' She stared at him, still stunned. 'Get a grip, Mark. This is me, Ginny, remember? Not one of your patients. And, if I've told you once I've told you a hundred times, Neil and I are just friends. Why can't you believe that?'

'I'm prepared to admit I've overreacted,' he said heavily, 'but things have not exactly been easy lately. You, me—us—and work.' One long finger reached out and stroked her cheek. 'I was worried. You wouldn't answer the phone and you looked terrible when you left the surgery. I suppose I wasn't thinking straight.'

His eyes were so dark she felt as if she could swim in them. She placed a hand to her stomach. 'I can look after myself.'

The finger that had been on her cheek touched her mouth. 'You don't sound very sure,' he said softly, his eyes dropping to her lips.

With no conscious thought she felt them part, heard her breath quicken. 'I'm very hungry,' she said huskily. 'I have to eat more vitamins. And more minerals. I probably need supplements. Mark, I don't think—'

'Shh.' The finger stilled her words. 'I'm not doing anything.'

But he was. Just his nearness was doing all sorts of things to her. She was burning hot, her mouth was aching and her limbs felt heavy and limp. She let him take the half-eaten banana from her fingers, waiting silently while he put it aside, completely unable to move.

Numbly she let his fingers move across her skin, mesmerised by him, her eyes barely open, and for a few punishing seconds he hesitated, almost as if he was about to pull away. Instead, with a gratifying groan, he reached for her, moving aside the hand that shielded her abdomen and lifting her urgently into his arms.

She went willingly, the wave of need for his touch overwhelming.

His mouth grazed her cheek and her throat, teasing, tormenting. He ignored the frustrated demands of her mouth until finally she buried her hands in his hair, forcing him back to her. The deep male taste of him awoke a craving she'd been trying to bury for weeks, but then it seemed as if a shadow came down between them, and she felt as if she weren't really there...as if she were dreaming.

She fought the feeling, struggled against it, but it thickened. She could feel Mark, she wanted him, but it didn't seem real. She pushed back, arching her body away from him and struggling to understand what was happening to her. She could hear a dim rushing sound, as if a train was passing. Abruptly, the room spun, her vision shifted and blurred, then there was nothing but cool darkness.

When she woke she was on her bed and her legs were propped up on a mound of pillows. Mark was sitting beside her, holding her wrist, with his head lowered, clearly checking her pulse.

With her free hand she gripped the sheet that covered her, pulling it higher to conceal the swell of her breasts which were visible where her blouse had become unfastened. 'What happened?'

'You fainted.' He lifted his head and released her arm. His voice was light but even in the lamplight she could see the concern in his eyes—that and the shrewd observation of her movement with the sheet.

She felt heat flood her face. What had nearly happened between them shocked her but she could understand it. They'd both been vulnerable. She'd had one of the most unsettling days of her life, her hormones were disturbed and he'd been upset—after all, he'd admitted he'd been worried about her all afternoon.

She licked her dry lips nervously. 'I've never fainted before,' she said quietly, 'but I haven't eaten much today.'

'So I guessed. Hence the bananas, hmm?' He frowned. 'Whatever you had to do in London must have been pretty important.'

Under his probing look she felt her face grow even hotter. 'I'm much better now,' she said shakily. 'I'll be all right.'

His mouth compressed. 'Meaning, please leave?'

She twisted the edge of the sheet in her fist. 'I'm very tired.'

'Fine,' he said briefly, his eyes hardening. He stood. 'Don't worry. I wasn't going to outstay my welcome.'

'Mark—I'm sorry!' Her voice rose as he walked away.

'I'm sure you are,' he said grimly. She heard the sound of him on the stairs, then heard him pause. A few seconds later he was back in her doorway again, his eyes cool. 'Call me if you need anything, and don't come in tomorrow if you're still unwell. There's nothing decent in your cupboards so I've ordered you some of the vitamins you were talking about—Jill from the pub should be here with broccoli and fish pie in a few minutes.'

\* \* \*

Ginny grimaced at her reflection in the bathroom mirror the next morning. She looked like something out of a horror movie. After eating the meal Mark had had delivered the night before, she'd felt too exhausted to do anything but sleep. Because she hadn't removed her make-up, her mascara had run, leaving grey stains around her eyes and across her cheeks. The streaks highlighted the drained pallor of her skin.

She smeared a moisturising cleansing cream across her face but her stomach contracted sickeningly at the smell and she gagged. Leaning forward, she tissued it off urgently, keeping her eyes squeezed shut until the sensation passed.

She groaned. Even if it hadn't lived up to its promise to take ten years off her appearance, the cream had cost her a fortune. She gave the bottle a disgusted look as she shut it away firmly in her cabinet. Regardless of the price, there was no way she was going to be able to use it just now.

She stepped under the shower and warily sniffed her shampoo, before lathering her hair. After a few minutes she rinsed the suds away, washed herself, then stepped out, towelling herself slowly, her energy levels—despite her best night's sleep in months—sapped by her nausea.

It wasn't easy to keep her expression calm when she encountered Mark as soon as she arrived at the surgery, but his words told her she'd probably managed. 'Back to normal, then?' he said quietly, holding the side door open for her.

She nodded. 'Fine.'

He passed her mail to her, before picking up his own from the receptionist. 'No irresistible impulse to dash off to London?'

She flicked blindly through the envelopes, concentrating on keeping her voice neutral although her senses responded urgently to his proximity. Her nausea was fading but the

memory of his embrace the night before was flustering her
again. 'I promise to be here all day.'

'No more dramatic collapses?'

'Oh, for God's sake!' The startled look she got from
Lynn as she breezed past with a welcoming smile was
enough for her to swallow her angry retort. 'Look, I'm
fine,' she muttered, adding more appeasingly, 'Thanks for
dinner. It was delicious.'

His mouth compressed. 'Make sure you eat a decent
lunch today.' He strode across to his office, leaving her
staring open-mouthed at his back.

Ginny finished her house calls before eleven so, as she
was in the area, she called in on Beryl Scott. Beryl seemed
delighted to see her and made her sit down. Her husband,
Bill, made them a pot of tea, before disappearing back to
his garden. 'Oh, I'm much better,' Beryl said happily, nodding down towards the foot that was concealed by crêpe
bandages and a slipper. She poured their drinks. 'It was
worth that long stay to make sure this old foot healed up
well and truly this time.'

Ginny accepted her cup with a smile of thanks and took
a sip of the steaming liquid. Beryl had been out of hospital
almost a month now, but the district nurse had been checking her dressings and until this week she'd been attending
Bryan's outpatients' clinic so Ginny hadn't caught up with
her. 'They treated you well, then?'

She nodded. 'That Mr Gould is such a nice man. Came
to see me every day, he did.'

She smiled. 'He's an excellent surgeon.'

'He said I was very lucky to have you as my GP,' Beryl
announced proudly.

'I'm sure he says that to all his patients,' Ginny said
lightly, before swallowing another mouthful of hot tea. 'He
wants more referrals.'

The elder woman chuckled. 'Well, he deserves them,

that's all I'll say, but I still think your surgery is wonderful. I don't know Dr Reynolds very well, but the one time I had to call him out at night he was very pleasant. He couldn't have been more charming.'

Charming wasn't a word she'd have used for Mark lately, Ginny thought privately, gritting her teeth. Irritable, demanding and confusing were the words that came to mind. 'How's the diabetes?'

'Six this morning. Once the foot cleared up my sugars came down again, just like you said.'

'Good.' After they'd finished their drinks she followed Beryl into her bedroom and examined her foot. 'Beautiful,' she said, applying a fresh protective dressing and replacing her slipper. 'They've done a good job.'

Her patient nodded. 'He said he can't guarantee I won't get more problems later but at least I'm all right for the time being.'

Ginny nodded, glad that Bryan hadn't been too optimistic with Beryl. Her diabetes meant she'd always be at risk of infections and there could be no guarantees about the future. 'Give the practice a call if you've any worries,' she said, as her patient opened the front door for her. 'I'm always happy to call round if you can't make it in.'

'Bless you, Doctor.'

Beryl lived on the opposite side of the village to the surgery, and on her way back through Ginny stopped at the tiny health-food shop an enterprising young woman had set up in a building that had once housed a bakery.

Sadly, the baker, one of her patients, had gone out of business recently. One of the consequences of the change in the villagers' shopping habits towards a once-weekly shop at a huge, modern supermarket several miles away had been the steady loss of businesses from the village itself, but the girl who was in charge of the health-food shop seemed enthusiastic and capable. Ginny hoped people would appreciate the service she was providing.

As well as a big basket of organically grown vegetables, she bought a salad roll full of the sort of nutritional things she needed for her baby. She ate the roll at her desk while she read through her mail and checked the morning's delivery of laboratory results. There was nothing that needed urgent attention. She initialled the sheets and dumped the pile into the filing tray, then glanced through the small sheaf of X-ray reports from the local hospital. Three recent antenatal ultrasound scans, all normal and all confirming dates she'd already calculated.

Ginny lifted her head and stared blankly at her closed door, wondering how it would feel to have her own scan and to see her own child for the first time. Conscious that she was smiling foolishly, she wondered who the baby would most look like. Her family or Mark's? Or would it be an even mixture of them all?

Her clinic that afternoon finished relatively early and she was sorting through her files, trying to decide what paperwork could wait and what needed doing urgently, when Mark interrupted. He barked at her so suddenly she jumped. 'Lynn said you were finished. Why are you still here?'

She turned around quickly, her eyes wide. 'What?'

'I'm on call,' he said flatly, 'so I'll cover the surgery. You look exhausted. Go home.'

'But there's loads of paperwork waiting. I didn't do any yesterday—'

'It'll wait.' He collected her coat from its hook and thrust it towards her, forcing her to take it. 'Come on, Gin. Home-time.'

He was right about her being tired and Ginny relented. She picked up her bag and walked though the door he held open for her.

'Make sure you eat something decent,' he said, just before she opened the side door into the car park. 'You're getting too thin.'

Not for long, she thought faintly, mercifully suppressing the hysterical giggle that threatened to bubble from her lips. She'd be huge soon. And then how would he react?

# CHAPTER SEVEN

GINNY knew at eight the next morning that she wasn't going to make it into the surgery in time for her first appointment. Now that she understood she was pregnant, all her symptoms seemed to have gone into overdrive. Her stomach still aching from retching, she reached for the telephone.

She explained to their receptionist that she'd be late. She asked if Lynn was in so she could ask her to arrange for Mark to see her first patients.

'She's not here yet. Oh. Wait a minute.' There was the sound of a muffled conversation and then Mark's voice.

'Ginny, what's wrong?'

She groaned. 'Nothing. I'm just running late.'

'Where are you?'

'At home.'

'Are you sick?'

Not as in illness, she thought irritably, raising her hand to her mouth to stifle the spasms. 'I'm fine,' she said urgently. 'I'll be there in an hour.' Without waiting for him to reply, she slammed down the receiver and dashed back to the bathroom.

She hadn't been in her office two minutes when he came in. 'Where were you?'

She swallowed, her eyes dropping to the hands that had once caressed her. 'I told you, I was at home.'

'I called you back. All I got was that bloody machine.'

'I heard you,' she said shortly, 'but I was busy.'

'Busy?'

115

'Look, I'm sorry, all right?' She was sitting so stiffly her back was starting to ache. 'I couldn't help it but I don't make a habit of being late.'

'I'm aware of that.' He sat on the edge of her desk, studying her as if she were an interesting sort of insect, his arms folded. 'That's what worries me.'

She slid back in her seat, fighting the urge to squirm away. He was too close and too aggressively male. 'Mark, I've work to do.'

'Are you sleeping?'

She blinked. 'Sleeping?'

'Yes, sleeping.' He frowned. 'Trouble getting to sleep or early waking?'

'I—I have been a little restless,' she conceded, suppressing the memory of dreams that always left her damp and flushed—dreams haunted by the image of the man in front of her.

His eyes narrowed. 'Just as I thought. You're depressed. I want you to go and see Philip.'

Mutely she put her hand to her head. This was going too fast for her. She wasn't depressed. Why should she see her GP?

He stood, pacing to the other side of the room. 'You've plenty of symptoms. Poor appetite, weight loss,' he recited, counting them off on his fingers. 'Poor sleep, altered mood, somatic symptoms, bizarre behaviour—'

'What?'

'Window-shopping,' he said scornfully, swinging to face her again. 'You've never window-shopped in your life.'

'You're being ridiculous.'

He ignored her. 'Your squash game.'

'How dare you call that bizarre? You play squash every—'

'Ginny, I've known you since you were nineteen. Until

that game I have never, never, seen you play any sport. Suddenly you start. Yes, I call that bizarre.'

'But—'

He didn't let her finish. 'Recent bereavement.'

She gulped. 'What?'

'Neil,' he said flatly.

'Oh, for God's sake!'

'Denial.'

'Will you shut up?' She surged out of her chair and glared up at him, her hands on her hips. 'You're mad. I'm no more depressed than...than Lynn!' she finished triumphantly. 'You're so experienced, so skilled, aren't you, Mark? So completely confident you're always right. Yet, despite all that, you've completely ignored the fact that we forgot...' She faltered.

'What—?'

'You take too much for granted,' she said quickly. 'You can't storm in here and start telling me what to do. You have no right to behave like this, no right at all, and don't think I don't realise you've still got the keys to my flat. I want them back or I'm having my locks changed and charging it to you.'

He just tilted his head, refusing to be diverted. 'What have we ignored?'

She lowered her head into her hands. 'Nothing. Leave me alone.'

'Ginny,' he growled.

'*Nothing*. I didn't mean anything.' She said each syllable grittily, although the words were muffled by her hands.

'Stop fighting me.' She heard him move and when she twisted the chair around he was there in front of the window, watching her, his face dark. 'Tell me what's wrong. I might be able to help.'

'Hardly,' she said grimly. He'd done more than enough already.

'Try me.'

One brief look at his set expression told her he wasn't going to give up and finally she sighed, acknowledging that she wasn't even sure if she wanted him to. Carefully, she pushed back her chair and sat on the edge of her desk, facing him. She'd planned to wait a few weeks, planned to give their relationship time to improve, but he had a right to know and this would give him more time to prepare. 'I'm amazed you haven't guessed already,' she said quietly. 'Really, I'd have expected you to think of it before me even.'

'Don't tell me you're marrying Donald?' His mouth twisted. 'That would add a nice surreal absurdity to this whole bloody mess.'

'Idiot.'

'Then tell me, Ginny.' His face was shadowed but there was no mistaking the irritation in his voice. 'What the hell is going on?'

'You should sit down.'

'Trust me,' he grated, not budging. 'However bad, *I* won't collapse.'

'Mark…' She didn't know how to say it and she stared at him, willing him to guess, but her hesitation only seemed to increase his frustration.

'Ginny,' he growled.

'I'm pregnant.'

There was an instant of stunned, silent shock then Mark sagged back against the ledge. He swore. 'I don't believe it.'

'It's true.' She leaned forward but with the light streaming in behind him she couldn't make out his expression. 'I fail to see why you're so surprised. It is one of the side-effects of unprotected sex.'

'Don't.' His voice was quiet. Too quiet. 'You're sure?'

'Yes.'

'How long have you known?'

'Only a few days.'

'I thought you were on the Pill.'

That surprised her—they'd never talked about it before—and she frowned. 'Why?'

'You had them in your bag.' He spoke like an automaton. 'The next day. I meant to say something—I was going to ask you if you were taking anything so we could organise emergency contraception if you weren't—but then I saw the pills and I let myself be reassured. Remember? When you were looking for your car keys.'

She sagged slightly, remembering then that she'd tipped out the contents of her handbag. 'They were old ones,' she said slowly. 'I had them prescribed when I started seeing Neil but, as I've told you, we never…well…I never actually started taking them.'

'Oh.'

'I've not been involved with anyone in that way for quite a long time,' she added nervously.

'Oh.'

'And after…that night…' Her face was burning now. 'I realise it's hard to understand and completely stupid, but I've always been very irregular and I never…well, in truth I've always thought that I might even have trouble conceiving. I never even considered the possibility of pregnancy.'

'Oh.'

'I wish you wouldn't keep saying that.' She squinted into the sun. 'And stop looking at me like that. It's your fault too.'

There was a pause. 'I'm well aware of that,' he said dully. He turned to face the window, his back to her. 'What exactly would you like me to say?'

'I don't know.' She stared at his broad shoulders. 'Anything.'

'Have you made any…arrangements?' he asked carefully.

She froze. 'Arrangements?'

'You know what I mean.'

She swallowed. 'Mark—'

'Just tell me, Ginny.' He turned back to her, his eyes bleak. 'Was that why you went to London on Monday?' She started, shocked, but he didn't wait for her to decide on the words. 'So what role have you got planned for me in all of this? Do I get to pay for the termination?'

'No!'

'Well, I'm sure as hell not going to hold your hand through it.'

'I didn't ask you to.'

His mouth twisted. 'What, then? Or are you just telling me so I can feel part of the process, even though we both know that what I think won't make any bloody difference?'

'Mark, I'm having the baby.'

In other circumstances his astonished expression would have been comical. 'What?'

'You heard me.'

'You don't want children.'

'I've never said that.'

'But you always said your career…' He looked bewildered, and she could understand that—she'd been bewildered as well. 'You've never talked about them. I was always the one…you've never said you did want them,' he added hollowly.

'I…I didn't realise until recently how much I did,' she said shakily. 'I didn't say anything in case…in case it never happened. I didn't want you…anyone…to feel sorry for me, I suppose. But I want this baby very much.'

'God! I never expected…' But he didn't finish the sentence, just stood there.

'I want you to know I won't be asking a lot from you,'

she said quickly. 'I can manage on my current income but obviously if I, I mean we, if we decide on private schooling, that sort of thing, there's a possibility I may have to ask for some financial…' She faltered, realising he'd gone very still suddenly, extraordinarily still, and it was as if a shutter had come down across his face.

'I've arranged an appointment with our solicitor next Monday afternoon.' She was speaking very quickly now. 'I was going to go alone but since you know now I could change the time to the lunch-break and you could come too. For advice in the first instance, but then I thought we could draw up an agreement—'

'Ginny!' Although his teeth were gritted the word was practically a roar and she flinched as he slammed his fist into the wall. 'I could kill you.'

Her own fists clenched. She surged out of her seat and walked away from him to be close to the door. She'd never seen him like this and he was alarming her. She needed to know that she could get out if she had to. 'Everything will be fine,' she said jerkily. 'Calm down. This can be managed in quite a civilised—'

'I don't share your sense of civilisation,' he grated. 'What do you mean, you won't be asking much of me? And what the hell are you doing, calling in a lawyer?'

'So we'll both know exactly where we stand.'

'I know exactly where I stand,' he growled. 'You're pregnant with my child.'

'Mark—'

'Mark nothing.' He looked at his watch and swore, swore violently. 'You pick your times, Ginny Reid. You sure as hell pick your times. There's a waiting-room full of people out there.'

'You started this,' she snapped, stung.

'You could have said no,' he retorted, and she flushed.

They looked at each other and she knew he wasn't referring to this discussion.

Mark looked away first. He ran his fingers through his hair. 'Later,' he added, half-distractedly. 'We'll talk later.' He glared at her again. 'Cancel that appointment and don't waste any more time, making plans.'

When the door slammed behind him she walked mechanically back to her desk and stared blindly at the stacks of files awaiting her attention, willing her limbs to stop shaking.

A few minutes later her door opened. 'Ginny, it's after ten.' Lynn was regarding her with a concern that suggested she might have caught the sound of Mark and her, arguing. 'Are you ready for anyone?'

'Yes. Sorry. Of course.' She even managed a small, careless smile. 'Ever had one of those conversations where you're absolutely determined you're not going to row and then you open your mouth and suddenly it's war again?'

'Only every day with my children,' Lynn told her sympathetically.

'I don't know what's going to happen to us,' Ginny said weakly, her smile fading as despair drove her to confide where normally she sought privacy.

Lynn said, 'It's just work pressure, Ginny. The last few months have been bad. You both need a holiday. Even a few days away together would do you the world of good— get you talking again, like you used to. Before you know it things will be back to normal again around here.'

Ginny knew it wasn't that simple. 'I'll think about it,' she said huskily, standing up to call her first patient.

John Cleary, normally a robust, cheerful young man, looked tired and strained. He told her about his indigestion and abdominal pain and she forced herself to concentrate on his story. 'On and off for more than six months now,' he added. 'Cindy's been at me to come along but I kept thinking it'd go away on its own.' He shrugged ruefully. 'I've been home a lot lately. Putting on weight, with Cindy's cooking three times a day, and that's not helping.'

Ginny nodded, remembering that Lynn had told her some time ago that John was being made redundant. No doubt the stress of that had added to his problems. 'Have you tried anything for the pain?'

'Peppermint water and some tablets Cindy bought from the chemist. Don't remember the name but they tasted chalky.'

'Did they help?'

'For an hour or so. But the pain comes right back again. Here…' he rubbed his clenched fist up and down his sternum '…and sometimes here.' He indicated his epigastrium. 'Especially if I skip a meal.'

Despite the matter-of-fact way he'd described his pain, Ginny knew that he was the stoical type and she suspected that the discomfort was considerably worse than he'd described. She made sure that there was no family history of anything worrying, then examined him. He looked fit and there was no evidence of anaemia or tenderness in his abdomen. 'How are things on the work front?'

He didn't look surprised she knew about his redundancy. 'I've an interview next week that sounds promising.' He pulled his shirt back on. 'In Ipswich, mind, so it'll be a fair commute, but I suppose I could get used to it.'

Once he was dressed Ginny sent him across to Lynn for testing, and when she had a result Ginny called him back in to explain the diagnosis. 'The blood test Lynn just did is a little like a pregnancy test, only in your case it showed that you've been infected with a bug called *Helicobacter pylori*.' She smiled at his expression. 'Don't worry, the name's not important. What matters is that this bacteria lives in the stomach and small bowel and destroys the acid and causes ulcers.'

He looked relieved. 'Is that all it is, then? Ulcers?'

'Without asking a gastroenterologist to look down with a camera, I can't be sure,' she admitted. 'But I'm going to prescribe you a mixture of two antibiotics and an ulcer-healing drug, and if a course of that gets rid of both your pain and the bacteria then you won't need any further tests.' Seeing him brighten further, she warned, 'But if you're still having pain afterwards I'll have to refer you to a specialist for further investigations.'

'If it is this…helicopter thing, causing all the trouble, will these tablets cure me?'

'Nine out of ten that's all you need,' she confirmed, reaching for her prescription pad. 'Happily you don't smoke, but how much alcohol are you drinking?'

He shrugged. 'One or two pints on a Friday night plus a couple during the week—not a lot.'

'That shouldn't do you any harm.' She handed him the script for the three drugs she wanted, clarithromycin and amoxicillin and omeprazole, the combination suggested most recently in one of the GP journals the practice sub-scribed to. 'The course lasts a week but come back in a month or so and let me know how things are going.'

'Thanks, Dr Reid.' She noted that the strained lines around his mouth had relaxed and his voice was heartier. 'If I'd known it'd be this straightforward I'd have listened to Cindy and been along months ago.'

Ginny watched him leave, her thoughts returning to her own problems. Pity there weren't some magic tablets she could take which would make Mark gentle and amenable.

The instant her well-women's clinic finished that after-noon she hurried out of the surgery. She'd heard Mark greeting the receptionist when he returned from his calls a short time earlier and she was determined to avoid him. The wisest plan, she'd decided, would be to delay more discussion for as long as possible.

In order to stay out of his way, she'd eaten lunch very early so by the time she arrived home she was famished. She opened a carton of fresh mushroom soup, letting it heat while she grilled a slice of cheese on toast.

Her diet definitely needed attention, she realised. The groceries she'd bought the day before would help but she'd been careless until now. Working long hours, it had been too easy to rely on quick, ready-prepared meals that she could pop in the microwave. From now things had to change.

Ginny stared down at the steaming soup, her brow creasing as she thought about what harm she might have done to her baby over the past two months. She took vitamin tablets that contained folic acid sporadically but not as regularly as a woman should prior to conception and in early pregnancy.

What about that squash game? It had nearly killed her. She'd been stiff and sore for days afterwards. It was unwise to take up new, unaccustomed exercise in pregnancy—she could have miscarried. But she'd had dozens of patients who'd only found out they were pregnant many months after conception and she knew their babies had been healthy. Clearly the growing foetus was more hardy than she imagined.

Despite her training, it was hard to think about her own body with the rational objectivity of a doctor, and she was still preoccupied by worry as she carried her food to the table. Before she could begin to eat someone pounded on her front door. Within the few seconds it took her to get downstairs the impatient person had knocked again.

Mark scowled at her when she opened the door. 'Don't look so surprised. You knew I'd come.'

Mutely she turned and walked back up the stairs, hearing him close the door and follow her.

'This is dinner?' He gave her meal a disdainful glare. 'You're supposed to be eating for two.'

'It's a sensible meal.' She glared up at him, resenting his size, his confidence and his air of healthy maleness. She resented everything about him, in fact, particularly the forceful reminder of her body's consciousness of him that her sudden breathless flush gave her. 'Believe it or not, I have mastered the basics of human nutrition.'

He wasn't diverted by her sarcasm. 'You've lost weight,' he said bluntly. 'I've never seen you this thin.'

Ginny shifted under his frank gaze as he looked her up and down, feeling uncomfortably exposed despite the shield of her clothes. It didn't help that she remembered the way he'd looked at her naked body that night. His eyes hadn't been critical then. She folded her arms across her breasts, suddenly irritated with herself for being so easily distracted. She knew his tactics. He hadn't come here to discuss her weight. He was trying to disarm her before battle. 'What do you want?'

There was a shrewd gleam in the eyes Mark lifted back to her face, and Ginny knew he'd noted her protective gesture with her arms. 'Nothing complicated,' he said quietly.

As if sensing her tension, his mouth twisted and he seemed to relent. 'For starters, a drink,' he said flatly, striding towards her kitchen.

She perched on the edge of an armchair, her heart thudding loudly in her chest as she listened to him moving around.

He returned a few minutes later with the Scotch she kept for him, an empty glass and one full of an amber liquid. He handed her the full one. 'I opened an apple juice,' he said wryly when she wrinkled her nose. 'You were out of orange.'

'I've stopped drinking it,' she explained softly. 'Since

the baby…well, I think orange juice has been giving me reflux.'

'That's not uncommon.' He poured a generous measure of whisky and took a mouthful. 'Does anybody else know?'

She took a sip of her drink, not bothering to pretend she didn't know what he was talking about. 'No.'

He took the seat opposite her. 'Your mother?'

'Not yet.' Ginny was putting off calling Australia. 'You know what she'll be like,' she told him. 'She's old-fashioned about this sort of thing.'

Mark's mouth tightened but he didn't comment. 'We'll have to tell the staff.'

She looked down into her glass, frowning. 'Not now.'

'Yes, now. They have to understand I want your work-load reduced and no lifting.'

Ginny stiffened. 'If you think—'

'Yes, I think,' he said smoothly. 'I think I can interfere whenever I like. You're carrying my child.'

She surged out of her chair, too nervous to stay still. After a long, brittle silence she murmured, 'So, you do want it?'

'Of course I do.'

Considering he'd never said so, she decided his impatience was unwarranted and despite her relief she bristled. 'Then why all that fuss about the lawyer? A contract's a sensible solution. It'll protect both our rights as parents.'

He took a long swallow of his drink, watching her over the rim of his glass. 'The only contract we need is a wedding certificate.'

'I just knew you'd say something clichéd like that!' She spun back towards him. 'Obviously my mother's not the only old-fashioned one. The idea's ridiculous.'

As if her protest left him unmoved, his expression didn't change. 'You know it's best.'

'Rubbish. Lately we can't talk five minutes, without fighting. I'm not going to raise a child into that.'

'We've only fought since that night, and you know the reason for it,' he said calmly. 'Frustration's easily cured.'

'We fight because you're insufferable,' she snapped, hating his smugness.

'And unattached,' he said quietly. 'And solvent. And the father of your child.'

Her fists clenched. 'I don't want our child growing up, knowing we married because I accidentally got pregnant.'

'It doesn't have to be like that.'

'This is the nineteen-nineties,' she countered. 'Nuclear families are going out of fashion.'

'I'm not interested in fashions.'

'We'd be miserable. What about when you fall in love with some woman and want to get rid of me?'

'That won't happen.'

'Yes, it would. Apart from Sarah, when's the last time you went more than six months without changing girl-friends?' she demanded. '*Six*? Huh! Try, more than three. From our work you must know how traumatic divorce can be for a child.'

'Your first point is ludicrously exaggerated.' He lifted his glass and swallowed the last of the Scotch. 'If my sex life was as active as you've always seemed to have assumed, I'd never have finished med school. Anyway, that's as irrelevant now as your second point. There will never be a divorce.'

'Separation, then.' She glared at him, her hands on her hips. 'What you're talking about isn't a proper marriage—it's just pandering to society's expectations. It's your over-developed sense of responsibility talking and you're making a mistake.'

Then she stopped, realising that she was berating him like a shrew when he was only trying to do what he thought best. She spread her palms appeasingly towards him. 'I understand how you feel, and I appreciate the sentiment—you want what's best for all of us, and that's what I want too. But marriage isn't the solution. It would only create new problems. When you calm down you'll realise I'm right.'

His throat made a convulsive movement, but when he spoke it was quietly although with a loaded undercurrent which suggested he might be holding himself tightly in control. 'We'll sell this place and convert the small room upstairs in the house to a nursery. I'll cover your on-call nights, in the meantime, and we'll advertise for another partner to join the practice in time for your maternity leave. With the workload lately, we need another partner anyway so there'll be room if you decide to return part time after the baby.'

She leaned against the wall and drew a deep, shuddering breath, frustrated that he continued to ignore her. 'Mark, this does not make sense. Why can't you see that?'

His eyes on her stomach, he said, 'I've discovered I'm an extremely possessive man.'

'The baby's yours,' she grated. 'No one can take that away from you.'

He leaned back, crossing one leg nonchalantly over the other. His hands linked to form a pyramid, his eyes dark and narrowed. 'You don't care if I marry another woman?'

She pressed her back harder against the wall and the cold of the bricks leached through the cotton of her shirt. 'I... No.'

'Liar.' He spoke quietly but the word vibrated in the air between them and the gut-wrenching truth was that he was right.

Because a wife would mean he'd have less time for their child, she told herself. 'As long as your w-wife...' She stumbled over the word. 'As long as she loves our child, too,' she said fiercely, and met his gaze head on, refusing to admit his words had pierced her armour, 'then, of course, I'd want you to be happy.'

'The issue's not going to arise. We both know that you can make me happy—that we can make each other happy.'

'You're just talking about sex.' She shook her head in vigorous denial of the importance of that, even though the memories were burrowing under her skin like tiny worms. 'That's nothing.'

'Think harder,' he said softly, in that same persuasive, reasonable voice. 'We've lasted fifteen years together without sex so we can last a hell of a lot longer with it. We're good together.'

He was right but that didn't mean it would always be so. Ginny ground her back into the wall. 'You're not playing fair.'

'This is too important,' he said quietly, and the words hammered at her. 'You must have known I'd want this.'

'Your reaction's primitive.'

'I've never felt so strongly about anything in my life.'

She closed her eyes weakly. 'It wouldn't work.' The fact that he wanted their child was enough—it meant he'd always be there and that he'd be a good father and that was enough for her. If they married because of the baby she'd feel guilty for ever.

With brutal honesty she acknowledged that although she could easily spend her life with Mark—she knew him well enough to know that he offered everything she'd ever wanted in a husband—the flip side of agreeing to marriage would be that she'd always be wondering if he was regretting it and, because he was always honourable, if she was stopping him from finding supreme happiness with a woman he loved.

She wasn't good at hiding her emotions. Her doubt and guilt would eventually tear their relationship apart, leaving nothing but acrimony. She couldn't subject her child to that.

They had the best arrangement now: friendship with free-
dom and no obligation.

'What if I fall in love?' she asked defensively. Although
the idea of ever becoming involved with another man
seemed ludicrous, she was searching for something to divert him. 'It might happen. I might want to marry someone
else.'

Mark's eyes glittered dangerously. 'Neil?'

'No.' Ginny's teeth gritted. 'I mean later, in the future.'

'Now's all that matters. I want you living with me.'

Relieved that he'd switched from demanding marriage,
she said, 'Convert your garage to a flat.' Her flat would be
too small once the baby was older. His house was big
enough for all of them and it was a compromise she was
prepared to make. 'Or we'll share the house and do the
nursery, like you said. We'll work something out.'

His jaw tightened, but instead of the argument she started
bracing herself for he stood, stepped forward and took her
hand. 'Got any food?'

Ginny stiffened, her worried eyes probing the carefully
shuttered brown of his. 'Mark...'

'I heard you,' he said flatly. 'That's enough for now.'

'If you think—'

His hand stoppered her mouth. 'I'm not thinking of anything,' he said gently, 'but food. It's late and I missed
lunch.' He eyed her congealed plate doubtfully. 'Right now
even that appeals.'

She hesitated then finally took the olive branch he was
offering. 'Pasta with Ginny's original tomato sauce?'

'Infinitely better.' He smiled, the old, friendly, caring,
Mark smile that made her insides feel warm. 'Slices or
chopped?'

She found herself smiling at the memory of the little
ritual they used to share. It was months since she'd cooked

for him but Mark always cut the onions when she did. They never reduced him to tears as they did her.

They ate dinner quietly and afterwards he helped her wash up, teasing her as he used to about the care she took to inspect every dish carefully before she passed it over for drying, then grinning at her mock rage when he arbitrarily rejected items and dumped them back into the soapy water.

If they could preserve this sort of relationship, Ginny thought, they'd be able to cope with anything a baby could throw at them, but as she passed another soapy dish across and saw the way his fingers carefully avoided hers, she acknowledged that nothing was as relaxed as she was pretending. There was still that dark undercurrent between them, a silent awareness of him in her movements, a glitter in the depths of his gaze that made her awkward and a consciousness that they were both trying very hard to make this work.

After draining the sink, she dried her hands then said carefully, 'I was planning an early night tonight.'

He threw the damp cloth into her washing machine. 'Throwing me out?'

She flushed. 'It's late,' she said stiffly. 'And I'm on call tomorrow.'

He tapped the side of her cheek with a gentle finger. '*I'm* on call,' he said gently. 'I told you I'm going to cover you from now on.'

She dropped her gaze away from his steady one, focusing instead on the unfastened neck of his white shirt. He'd taken his tie off when he'd arrived, and the skin of his lower throat looked smooth and hard and warm. 'I don't want to argue about this, Mark.'

'Heaven forbid,' he muttered under his breath. She felt his hand at her chin, tilting her face, and reluctantly she lifted her eyes. 'Let me do this, Gin. I don't want you wearing yourself out.'

'Pregnancy's not an illness,' she said huskily. 'I can work.'

The creases between his eyebrows didn't go away. 'You know you never sleep properly when you're on call even if you're not woken. It isn't good for the baby.' Obviously realising she was about to object, he added impatiently, 'As a compromise, let me at least cover your first trimester plus, say, another few weeks. First and third, but most of the second you can do it. OK?'

She pulled her chin out of his grasp, immediately missing the warmth of his touch. 'I'll do my weekends.'

His mouth tightened. 'During the day,' he agreed finally. 'I'll do nights.'

'All right.' It wasn't much of a compromise—he would still be working most of her hours—but knowing he wouldn't back down and that life was infinitely simpler when he was happy she accepted his offer. 'Thanks.'

'You're welcome.' He leaned forward and kissed her cheek, a brief, light brush of a kiss that nevertheless had her legs trembling. 'Go to bed.'

'Yes.' She half lifted her hand but he was already at the door. Then there were just the sounds of his footsteps on the stairs and the door shutting downstairs. She walked to the living room and watched him through the curtains. She saw the long confident strides that propelled him across the road to his car, saw the athletic ease with which he climbed inside, saw him drive away from her with not even the briefest glance back towards her flat.

Ginny sank onto the edge of the armchair nearest the window, her face pale and strained. Having known Mark the lover, was she really going to be able to live contentedly with Mark the friend?

# CHAPTER EIGHT

GINNY rose early the next morning, hoping that way to be over the worst of her morning sickness before it was time to leave for work. As she stooped to peer at her miserable reflection in the bathroom mirror she vowed never again to dismiss the nausea her pregnant patients experienced by suggesting dry toast and basil-leaf tea. The thought of eating or drinking anything made her stomach churn.

She scrubbed her teeth and stepped under the shower, relishing the coolness of the hard spray against her flushed skin. Running an experimental hand over her flat abdomen, she registered a pang of sudden, urgent longing for the tiny creature that was making her feel so ill. Despite her knowledge of hormones and physiology, the life inside her still seemed like a miracle.

She was a little late, getting to work, and as she glanced up at the surgery as she locked her car she saw Mark, who was watching her from his office window. She lifted her hand casually but he didn't return the gesture, watching her steadily as she walked towards the building, his expression shadowed and brooding.

Suddenly uneasy, Ginny averted her eyes and tucked her bag nervously under her arm, fighting the childish urge to flee. The worst was over. He knew everything and they'd reached an understanding. They'd share a house, try their best to be friends again and he'd help her raise their baby. Life was going to be fine. Nothing could go wrong now.

Her first patient that morning was Michelle Parker, with her new baby, Sam. The protein Ginny had discovered in her urine two months earlier had been secondary to a minor infection which had cleared up quickly, causing no problems with the delivery which had gone exactly to plan.

'Breast-feeding's all right on the right,' Michelle said, unfastening her blouse and then her bra to show Ginny her reddened left breast, 'but this one's been sore since I left hospital. At first the nurse thought I wasn't emptying myself properly, but over the last week it's come up in a lump.' She winced as she showed Ginny. 'Here.'

Ginny popped a thermometer under Michelle's tongue, then gently probed the sore, fluctuant area just above her nipple. She checked the glands under her patient's arm which were swollen as well, and examined the opposite breast which, although tight with milk, was normal.

Allowing plenty of time for Michelle's temperature to register, Ginny washed her hands and took a look at Sam. He lay quietly in his pram. His big blue eyes blinked at her, his tiny fists clenched and his face screwed up, prunelike. She smiled. 'What a beautiful boy,' she said lightly.

Michelle's temperature was up. 'You've developed an abscess,' Ginny explained. 'It's not uncommon for the breast to get inflamed when you're breast-feeding. Doctors argue about whether it's because of a build-up of milk or purely an infection, but in the early stages antibiotics seem to work.'

Michelle nodded. 'So, more antibiotics?'

'It's a little too far gone for that,' Ginny said gently. 'Once there's an actual abscess like this the treatment is to make a small cut in the skin to release the pressure and let the build-up drain out. That means going to the hospital and seeing a surgeon,' she added, relieved at Michelle's resigned shrug. 'Hopefully you won't need to stay overnight.'

'Can I still feed Sam?'

'From the other breast,' Ginny confirmed. 'You'll need to express from the left.' She reached for the phone. 'Give me a few minutes to organise someone to see you and then you can call your husband. Is he back at work yet?'

Her patient nodded. 'But it's quiet this week so he'll be able to get off easily enough.'

When she got through to the surgical registrar on call Ginny explained Michelle's condition, and the registrar agreed to see her in Casualty. 'We'll try and incise it under local,' she told Ginny, 'but nothing to eat or drink in case she needs a GA.'

While Ginny had been on the phone Michelle had retrieved Sam from his pram, and Ginny took the baby so she could telephone her husband. Sam promptly squawked his objection so she took him into the back corridor, jiggling him to try and quieten him so that his mother could continue her conversation. As soon as she held him against her breast Sam quietened, and Ginny smiled down at his creased little face and the small seeking mouth that burrowed at her blouse.

Mark's door opened as she walked past and for a few seconds they both froze. 'He looks content,' he said quietly.

'Mmm.' She dropped her eyes to avoid the dark, probing depths of his. 'Considering how babies normally abhor me, perhaps it's my pregnancy. Perhaps I smell like a mother to him.'

Mark lifted one broad shoulder noncommittally. He stroked Sam's cheek. 'You won't find anything there,' he told him softly, his finger shifting to brush lightly back and forth across the nipple the baby had been seeking. 'Not yet.'

Ginny went rigid, stunned by the tiny fronds of heated sensation that radiated from where he was touching her. Her eyes flew to his face. 'Mark…'

'Hmm?' He was looking at her breast, not her face. Shockingly, for any of the nurses or receptionists could walk by at any time, he released one button of her blouse and slid his hand inside and beneath the lace of her bra to cup her breast, his thumb moving maddeningly over the taut centre. 'Will you breast-feed our baby?' he asked, backing her against the wall, his voice very low.

She looked down, watching the slow moments of his hand beside Sam's contented head. Her whole body quivered. She had no more strength to stop him than will. 'I...suppose so,' she whispered.

'You're swollen. Do they hurt?'

She swallowed. 'They're a bit...sensitive.'

His thumb chafed her slightly, made her lift, ache, gasp. 'Am I hurting you?'

'No.' It sounded like a plea and she realised it was. A plea for more.

Very slowly, his eyes still on her breast, he removed his hand and refastened her clothes. Then he looked at her, his dark eyes satisfied as he surveyed her flushed face. 'Good.'

Lifting his jacket off the rack by the door, he slung it over his shoulders. 'I've only three calls,' he said evenly. 'Shouldn't be late back.' Leaving her leaning against the wall, numb and trembling, he opened the side door and walked out.

Three hours later she was still shaking. She was susceptible to him, she'd known that already, but it stunned her that she'd been at work, with little privacy, holding a baby, but still had had absolutely no power to control her body's physical response to him. She jumped when her door opened suddenly, and looked up warily from the computer screen, but it was Lynn, not Mark, with a pile of repeat prescriptions for her to check and sign. 'This is one of Mark's patients,' she said, indicating the top one. 'Do you mind? Sorry, but she's waiting for it and he's still not back from his calls.'

Ginny signed it along with her own. 'I thought he only had three people to see?'

'He's probably dropped in on Nellie Jarvis,' Lynn told her. 'I saw her daughter, Sylvia, in the newsagent last night and she said he calls most days. After hours if he's too busy here.'

That sounded like Mark. Despite the fraught state of her emotions after what had happened that morning, she felt a familiar rush of warmth for his caring. 'How's Nellie this week?'

'She's not suffering.' Lynn took the scripts back, smiling her thanks. 'Sylvia says that now she's seen her precious roses start to bloom she's more at peace.'

When she was alone again Ginny walked to the window, pressed her forehead to the cool glass and closed her eyes. She remembered Mark's hand at her breast and her breath jammed in her throat. Her reasons for not giving in to him last night were good reasons, valid ones, yet her desire today had sapped at her control and, more disturbingly, Mark's satisfaction at her response suggested he understood his power.

She had a meeting with Miles, their practice manager, and Mark after work that afternoon to discuss an audit Miles had undertaken of their referral procedures. Although she felt embarrassed and anxious about facing Mark again, he seemed irritatingly relaxed, returning her nervous gaze coolly on the few occasions when she allowed her eyes to flick in his direction.

On Friday there was more of the same. Instead of alleviating her worries, his calmness added to her foreboding. She felt as if she had a pack of confident hounds looming behind but yet she didn't understand why.

In the early afternoon when Mark came to tell her he was leaving for his golf game she could barely bring herself to look at him. 'Fine,' she said, as crisply as she could manage. She kept her gaze fixed on her terminal, relief weakening her muscles as she realised there'd be no arguments for now. 'See you Monday.'

'Or perhaps earlier.' He'd spoken softly and when her eyes flew to his face in alarm she saw his cool observation and realised that he understood exactly how she was feeling.

'I'm on call this weekend,' he added. 'I might call by if it's quiet.'

'I'll be out. I'm thinking about going down to London.'

'I wouldn't bother.' He perched on the corner of her desk, his thighs inches away from her hands, forcing her to snatch them away in case he saw how they shook. 'There's nothing for you in London. Gin, stop worrying so.' One finger smoothed the creases in her forehead, then touched her cheek and slid lower to the corner of her mouth, sending heated shivers across her skin. 'It's bad for the baby and there's nothing you can do.'

'You're playing with me,' she whispered.

'Or perhaps I'm just courting you?' He rubbed gently back and forth across her lower lip, his eyes registering satisfaction at the involuntary parting of her lips, which occurred despite her best efforts to pull away. 'Don't you like it?'

'It won't work.'

'I think it might.' The finger drifted over her chin, over the sensitive skin of the neck she arched for him and probed the fastenings of her blouse.

'I'm my own person,' she whispered. 'I'm not going to give in to you about marrying. I won't let you bully me.'

'I don't want to bully you.' He half frowned and she saw that he'd read her panic with the same effortless ease with which he'd aroused her. 'I just want you to see reason.'

He eased himself from her desk and for a brief moment he looked down at her, watching the way her fingers scrambled to the buttons he'd undone. Finally he bent, eased her clumsy hands away and fastened them himself. 'Ginny, Ginny,' he chided patiently. 'What would you do without me, hmm?'

Abruptly she swung her chair away from him, pretending to study her terminal again, but his knowing look as he left her office told her there was little point in trying to deceive him. The balance of their relationship had swung vastly his way, she knew that. For years they'd been evenly matched but somehow now Mark seemed all-powerful and she didn't know how to deal with it.

'See you soon,' he said evenly, before closing her door.

But he didn't see her soon, and although Ginny spent much of her weekend preparing herself for an argument she still hadn't seen him by the time she arrived for work Monday.

Mrs Atkins, the mother of Warren, her patient with schizophrenia, was her first scheduled patient of the morning and she was waiting already so Ginny avoided the kitchen and went straight to her office to see her.

'You're looking the best I've seen you in years,' Ginny told her approvingly, writing out the prescription Mrs Atkins had requested for something to settle her stomach in case she got sick on the package holiday she was taking to Spain the following week. 'Warren must be enjoying his new job, then.'

'Started last week,' she was told with a quick nod. 'Thank you for all your help, Doctor. The letter you wrote got it for him, I'm sure. Employers are usually a bit nervous, you know, with psychiatric problems like his, but they decided he was best for the job.'

'Warren's always been a good worker. I'm just glad he's feeling up to it again.'

'Oh, he's so much better.' Mrs Atkins smiled. 'That time in hospital really sorted him out. They've given him new pills—without all the side-effects, they said. I think he's happy with them.'

'Good.' Ginny handed her the script. 'And his new employer doesn't mind about him taking time off for a holiday?'

There was a short, startled silence. 'Oh, Warren's not coming,' she said, adding quickly, 'Unless... You do think he's well enough now to be on his own for two weeks?'

'Of course he is. If you like, I'll stop by one evening and make sure he's not just eating junk food.' Ginny was intrigued. In all the time she'd known the family, Mrs Atkins had never gone anywhere on her own. 'So you're going with...?'

'With Raymond,' the elder woman said firmly, but Ginny could see that she was blushing now. 'Just the two of us. For two weeks.'

'That's wonderful.' Ginny smiled. 'I didn't even know you'd been keeping in touch.'

Mrs Atkins looked pleased with herself and she lowered her eyes, tucking the script away carefully in her handbag. 'We weren't. But I thought it was only fair to let him know when Warren went into hospital again. He went to visit him, you know, before he was discharged. Just to say hello, a fatherly thing. I think he was surprised at how normal he was. And then we got to talking. And then...' She lifted one frail shoulder hesitantly. 'Well we thought a holiday would do us both good.'

'I think it'll be fantastic.' Ginny walked with her to the door. 'I'm very pleased. Send me a postcard if you get time.'

'I will.' She nodded. 'Thank you, Doctor.'

'You're very welcome.' Ginny watched the little woman leave the surgery, realising she felt a little weepy suddenly. Hormones again, she told herself.

Her next patient was Michelle Parker, back for a dressing

check after her breast abscess had been opened and drained at the Norfolk the previous week.

'They had to put me to sleep,' she told Ginny cheerfully. 'They said it went too deep to do with the local.'

Ginny was concentrating on taking down the dressing. 'That's sometimes the way. Much pain?'

'Not much at all. Sam's dad came in and looked after him while I was in the operating theatre and they brought him straight back afterwards and we went home that night. There was a drain but they took that out the next day. It's just about healed now, I think.'

Ginny peeled back the final layer of dressing carefully to reveal a small, clean wound. 'You're right,' she said encouragingly. 'It looks fine. In fact, you can leave it exposed now. Don't worry about another dressing.'

While Ginny washed her hands Michelle dressed and retrieved Sam from his pram. 'I've been expressing the milk from that side. Can I start feeding directly again now?'

'Yes.' Ginny clicked her tongue softly at Sam. 'He's growing quickly, isn't he? I can see the difference even in a few days.'

'Dr Reynolds came and said hello to him when we were in the waiting-room. He said Sam was the handsomest baby in town.' Michelle was obviously delighted by Mark's praise. 'He says he's got footballer's legs. That'll please his dad. He's already bought him an Ipswich hat and he wants me to get the full set made.'

Ginny smiled at the image of the tiny baby dressed in football regalia. 'Lucky your husband's not a racing fan,' she said lightly. 'The rate he's growing he's going to be jockey size by the time he's two.'

Her clinic that morning was crowded and Mark obviously had a similar load because she still hadn't seen him when it was time to leave for her half-day. She collected her things and told one of the receptionists she was leaving, but as she walked back through the now-empty waiting-room towards the door Lynn called to her. 'Sorry, Ginny,' she said urgently. 'I forgot. Neil called earlier but you were examining someone so I told him you'd ring back. He knew it was your half-day and he said something about meeting up if you had some free time.'

Ginny's brow creased as she wondered why he wanted to meet. She hadn't heard from him in weeks and had assumed he was too busy, seeing the woman Mark had mentioned.

Lynn added, 'There's still room for him at the practice dinner on Thursday if he's interested.'

'Neil's not keen on Chinese,' Ginny said vaguely.

'Lynn?' They both jumped and swung around at Mark's command. He was standing in his open doorway, watching them, and Ginny had no idea how long he'd been there. 'Would you come in here and fix this dressing before you take lunch, please?'

As the nurse bustled across he looked at Ginny. 'Can we talk?'

Her heart thudded. 'Can't it wait?' she said tightly. She held up her bag. 'I'm on my way home.'

His mouth compressed. He closed his own office door behind Lynn and walked across to hers, holding it open. 'Just a few minutes.'

Her legs felt like stiff iron bars but she walked over, giving him a wary look as she passed into her office. Still holding her bag, she turned, leaned against the desk and waited.

He closed the door. 'So Neil's fling is over,' he said, almost musingly. 'I don't want you seeing him.'

Ginny tilted her chin. 'I can meet who I like.'

'If you don't cancel I'll do it for you.'

'This is absurd.'

Mark smiled but there was no amusement in the movement. 'I've let you play it your way long enough,' he said flatly. 'All you're doing is wasting time, Gin. There's no reason not to get married so let's just get on with it.'

'Then spend the rest of our lives regretting it?' She walked directly over to him, daring him with her eyes to try and stop her leaving, but he leaned back against the door with deliberate relish and effortlessly captured the wrist she raised to him.

'Church or register office? Any preference?'

'A few months ago you were telling me you couldn't promise anything about the future—and that was when we were just contemplating sex,' she hissed. 'How can you now say a marriage would last?'

'Things have changed.'

'I haven't.'

'No, you're still just as stubborn,' he said evenly.

'Believe it.' She jerked her arm out of his grip.

'And just as gorgeous and just as desirable.'

The dark intensity of his gaze should have offended her, should have angered her, but instead it made her suddenly weak and breathless. 'Mark...don't...'

'Remember how it was?'

'I can't forget,' she said hoarsely. 'Why are you doing this to us? I thought we'd agreed to share the house and try and get along—'

'I'm not interested in having you as a *boarder*.'

'That's all right.' She took a deep, calming breath, then said weakly, 'I've decided that it would be ridiculous to try and keep the arrangement platonic.'

She lifted her eyes and met his, wondering if the bleakness of his gaze—where she'd expected triumph—meant that he was thinking of what he'd given up with Sarah.

For a few seconds neither of them moved, then he shifted abruptly, turned and wrenched out her chair. She walked towards him and sat down and he pulled the wooden chair normally used by her patients around so he sat across from her, the desk to one side.

'Then there's no reason not to marry immediately.' His voice was laced with steel. 'I'll make the arrangements.'

She tried to push herself out of her chair but his hands on the arms stopped her, and all she succeeded in doing was bringing herself closer to his hard face. He was close now, very close, so close she could see the play of vivid copper within the black-brown of his eyes.

'The baby's only secondary, Ginny. It was the sex that changed everything. I want you.' The words were warm against her skin. 'You know that. I want to be there,' he intoned softly, 'all the time. I want to watch you feed our baby, I want to be there when you sleep and I want to be there when you wake—and you know exactly how that feels because you feel the same.'

'Yes.' Her chest felt so constricted she could barely breathe but she forced herself to stay rational. 'You're right. I can't stop thinking about you...about that...but it won't last for ever. I know you, Mark. I've watched you for years. One day you'll meet a woman who affects you like Sarah, and even though you won't say anything I'll know you want to leave.' Ignoring the denial she could see on his face, she forced herself to continue. 'Be rational. Think of yourself,' she said urgently. 'If we're married it'll be difficult...'

He spread his legs and pulled her chair closer with sheer brute strength so that although she tried to draw back his mouth was at her ear. 'I want you in my bed. I want to be with you. I want to taste you.' He held her when she tried to twist away, her body tortured by the soft, insistent words. 'I want to marry you.'

'But you don't love me!'

'Is that important?' His mouth caressed her ear and he bit softly at her lobe. 'Are you saying you love me?'

'No! I don't know.' She shook her head, evading his mouth's intimate invasion. 'Yes, sometimes. Always like a friend. But there are times when I hate you. Stop it. It's still not right.'

'Yes, it is.' He lifted his head, watching her now, his satisfaction warning her that he saw the way she wavered— seduced by his acknowledgement of the same desire as the one which was tearing her apart. If he wanted her as powerfully as she wanted him, perhaps it might work. If his desire really was that strong then she could make him happy, couldn't she? For the sake of their child, wouldn't they be able to make this work?

Abruptly he slid his hands beneath her and lifted her from her chair onto his lap so that she straddled him. 'We're going to give our child the most stable upbringing possible,' he muttered, nuzzling her cheek and the eyelids that closed for him. 'You know a proper family provides the optimum environment for a child to grow up in. Say yes.'

She tipped her head back. 'We'll live together.'

'I'm not leaving you free to take my child away if things get rough.'

His voice came from far away, barely audible over the pulse that thudded in her ears. 'Will that be when you stop wanting me?' she managed to whisper, between the soft gasps that rose involuntarily from her mouth.

She felt the cool brush of air as he unfastened her blouse, then the rush of heat as he bared one breast and lifted her against him, lowering his mouth. 'Forget that,' he murmured. 'Forget everything but this and tell me yes.'

His mouth closed over her and she groaned, her head falling back further as she arched, her fists clenching in his hair. 'Yes. Of course.'

He lifted his head again, surveying her flushed and weak

submission, and his dark eyes gleamed with triumph. 'Call Neil,' he rasped, dragging the phone across. 'Cancel.'

Her eyes locked with his, she took the receiver from his hand, looking away only briefly to stab out the numbers. As soon as the ringing tone stopped, Mark bent his head to her breast again.

'Neil, it's Ginny,' she said unsteadily, her breath catching as Mark's hands slid around her hips. 'I got your message but I can't…meet this afternoon.'

'Oh, well, never mind.' He sounded quite cheerful. 'I've some good news. How about tonight?'

'No…not tonight.'

Mark captured her wrist with one hand when she wriggled, trying to fend him off.

'Perhaps…tomorrow?'

'No, not tomorrow,' she said breathlessly, her voice rising as Mark's hand slid provocatively to the edge of her skirt. 'Neil, I'll call you, OK? I'm sorry. I have to go.'

Not waiting to hear Neil's response, she let the receiver drop but Mark caught it and replaced it. Ginny met his dark eyes and shivered at their glitter. 'You're sick,' she whispered.

'I should make you call Donald,' he said rawly, not denying her accusation. 'That might exorcise a few demons.'

Her entire body flushed from the heat that spread from his hand on her thigh. 'You need help,' she muttered. 'That's obscene.'

'That's revenge.' He lifted her forward and kissed her hard, then returned her to her chair. 'It's almost two,' he muttered when she blinked at him, stunned by the withdrawal of his touch. 'I'm keeping people waiting.'

Avoiding his shrewd gaze, she tried to straighten her clothes, uncomfortably aware that she'd have let him make love to her regardless of where they were, aware also that he'd achieved everything he'd wanted.

Despite her doubts, she acknowledged that unless he changed his mind himself she was too weak to resist him now. She wanted him too much to fight him when he was so determined. She smoothed her hair with one shaking hand. 'Wh-when...' She cleared her throat. 'When did you think...?'

'I'll organise it,' he said, his voice firm where hers had quivered. 'And I'll tell you.'

Fine. She took a deep breath and expelled it heavily.

'We'll tell everyone now.'

'No!' She wasn't ready for that yet. 'Not now, please.' The suspicious narrowing of his eyes made her rush on. 'Give me a few weeks to get used to the idea myself then we'll tell everyone—do it properly.'

'A little time,' he confirmed quietly, 'but not much.'

'Yes.' She bent stiffly and collected her bag. 'Yes, OK.' For a few seconds she stared vaguely up at him, waiting for him to do something more, say something more. When he stayed silent she turned towards the door that opened into the back corridor, still too flustered to risk seeing Lynn or any of the others.

He opened the door for her. 'Stop worrying,' he told her, following her out through the side door into the car park. 'It's not good for you.' He took the keys from her hand, opened the door to her car and waited for her to climb inside.

She lowered her window when he'd shut the door. 'What I said...about it not being platonic?' she asked huskily, the words trembling in her throat. 'Tonight?'

He stilled. 'After the wedding.' He stroked one of her cheeks, still flushed from her question, his fingers brushing her hastily lowered lashes. 'Relax, Ginny,' he chided. 'No more stress. Think of the baby. Concentrate on resting and eating well.'

How could she when all she wanted to do was concentrate on how much she wanted to be with him? As she looked up at him, hunting for the courage to tell him, he withdrew his hand and straightened. 'Home,' he said firmly.

Possibly because of the humid, stormy weather, her Thursday morning clinic that week was hectic, with more than half the patients complaining of hay fever or asthma. Ginny was sure she was seeing more sufferers of both every year and she suggested to Lynn that they organised an audit of the statistics.

Directly after showing out her last patient, she had to rush off on her home visits and she didn't get back to the surgery until after two, by which time there were already several people waiting.

Normally she'd have skipped lunch but she didn't just have herself to think about now so she gulped down a sandwich between cases, and by way of punishment suffered uncomfortable burning behind her sternum all afternoon. Clearly indigestion was going to be a significant feature in her pregnancy. Terrific.

Towards the end of her clinic Lynn called her from Reception. 'Ginny, Mr Heath from the old Rectory is calling about his wife. I know he's too late for a routine visit but I think this might be urgent.'

'Put him through,' she instructed, mouthing an apology to the person she was seeing and greeting the elderly man when he was connected. 'What's the problem, Mr Heath?'

'It's the wife's eye, Doctor.' He sounded concerned. 'She doesn't want me to bother you but she's in a lot of pain and I've lost patience with her. We've been clearing out the cellar for a few days, carrying the old things up to the shed, only this morning when she went down the bulb blew and she got stuck in the dark until I got there. The eye's been hurting ever since. We washed it out with plenty of water and she put herself to bed but that was more than two hours ago now and it's worse than ever. It looks very red but she can hardly open it now. Do you think there could be some dust still stuck in there?'

'Has she had any trouble with her eyes lately?'

'I think she has a bit on and off,' he told her. 'A bit hazy now and then, she's told me.'

'How's her vision at the moment?'

'Not very good, I suspect.'

'Mr Heath, I'm going to come around straight away,' Ginny said quietly, keeping her tone deliberately reassuring. 'Tell Mrs Heath to keep resting and I'll be there within ten minutes.'

She quickly tidied up her current consultation, someone simply requiring a work certificate for another fortnight off work following recent surgery, collected her things, asked Lynn to apologise to the two patients still waiting to see her and to ask Mark to see them if they didn't want to wait until she got back, then dashed out to her car.

Mrs Heath was clearly in a lot of pain. She lay in a darkened room, her normally robust and healthy face drawn and pale and her right eye swollen shut. It felt hard and when Ginny managed to coax it open it was very red and the pupil was dilated and the cornea cloudy.

'This looks like glaucoma,' she said gently, once she'd confirmed the history, which included Mrs Heath seeing fuzzy halos around lights for a few weeks. She retrieved the plastic vial of pilocarpine she always carried in her bag for emergencies. 'That simply means that the fluid circulation inside your eye has blocked off and the pressure's built up. I'm going to pop in some eye drops and give you an injection for the pain, but you'll need to go up to the hospital to see an eye specialist.'

Mr Heath was hovering worriedly but he waited until Ginny had instilled the drops before saying, 'Does this mean an operation, Doctor?'

'Probably on both eyes to stop the same thing happening on the other side.' She squeezed Mrs Heath's hand reassuringly, but her patient merely nodded weakly in apparent relief that her pain would be short-lived. 'It's not a big operation but it's vital to fix the drainage system.'

Seeing how shocked Mr Heath looked, she added gently, 'Go and pack some things, Mr Heath. A coat and a nightie and toothbrush and toothpaste and some soap and a gown.' He didn't look capable of driving so she added, 'I'll drive you both into town myself to save waiting for an ambulance.'

'Are you sure you can't take care of her at home, Doctor?'

'She must go to hospital,' Ginny said firmly, electing not to increase his anxiety by pointing out that the alternative was blindness.

'He's frightened,' Mrs Heath rasped once he'd shuffled away. 'He hates hospitals. When I went in for the children he used to meet me in the garden outside at visiting time.'

'I shouldn't think you'll need to stay in very long.' Ginny had her bag open now. She drew up a small dose of morphine and added an ampoule of Stemetil to counteract any nausea. 'Has he had a bad experience?'

'His mother died in a TB sanatorium when he was quite young.' Holding one hand cupped protectively over her painful eye, she rolled onto her side so Ginny could give her the injection. 'Will it take long to work?' she gasped.

'Just a few minutes,' Ginny soothed, brushing her dress back into place. 'May I use your phone to call the hospital?'

'Of course.'

When Ginny returned to the bedroom, after speaking to the registrar on call for eye admissions, she saw that her patient looked marginally less pale. She helped her to her feet. 'Lean on me,' she instructed, and collected her bag, before guiding Mrs Heath out of the house and towards her car. She nodded her thanks when Mr Heath rushed to open the door. 'Traffic's light going in at this time of day so it shouldn't take us long.'

Mr Heath waited doubtfully beside her car once he'd cleared the door, although his wife was inside. He wrung his hands, obviously torn between worry about her and his fear of hospitals.

'I think you should come,' Ginny said calmly. 'It's up to you, of course, but at least that way you're together. I think you'll worry more here on your own.'

'If it gets too bad you can wait in the garden,' Mrs Heath told him weakly. 'Get in, Harry. We're in a hurry.'

Wordlessly he obeyed but there was a brief delay while Ginny instilled another dose of pilocarpine drops into Mrs Heath's eye—the registrar had suggested repeated doses to help open up the eye's drainage channels—and midway into town she pulled off the road and repeated the medication.

At the hospital Mr Heath came inside with them but he looked so stricken that Ginny waited with the couple, rather than rushing back to the surgery. The registrar who came to see them, though, was superb, calm and professional and so reassuring and matter-of-fact that she could see Mr Heath's anxiety easing. After having a quick word with the other doctor about her concerns, she felt happy about leaving them to his care.

Driving back to the village, the traffic was awful. As well as being rush hour, there'd been some sort of bingle on the dual carriageway and a lane had been closed off. Soon after clearing that she had to slow again for roadworks. She rapped her fingers against the steering-wheel, having been slowed once more as she approached the village by a heavy vehicle, hoping that Mark had been able to see her remaining patients so they were not still waiting for her.

Ginny arrived finally at the surgery tired and irritated and not at all in the mood for the discussion she was planning to have with her partner. She'd hardly seen him since Monday but thoughts of him and the baby and this supposed marriage had filled her head and there were things they needed to discuss, including the fact that Lynn had spoken to Sarah at the hospital earlier in the week and that apparently she was leaving for Scotland tomorrow afternoon.

Tonight she and Mark and the rest of the staff would be attending the annual dinner they shared with Donald's practice, and because several doctors from the hospital were coming as well there'd be too many people around for her to be able to talk privately with Mark. It had to be now.

The waiting-room was empty but his car had still been in the car park so she tapped on his door and opened it, looking broodingly at the dark head bent towards his computer screen. 'We have to talk.'

'Fine.' His voice distracted, he didn't even look up from his terminal. 'How's Mrs Heath?'

'Glaucoma, as I suspected, and she'll probably have surgery tonight,' she said crisply. 'Mark—'

'So it's been caught in time to save the vision?'

'The registrar was quite confident.' She glared at him—he still hadn't even glanced at her. 'Thank you for seeing my patients,' she said tightly, each word carefully controlled.

Finally, as if sensing her mood, he looked up. 'What are you worrying about now?'

'This marriage thing is ludicrous,' she said angrily. 'Let's just have sex and get it out of our systems.'

# CHAPTER NINE

MARK sighed, then abruptly shoved his chair back and stood to face her. 'I don't want any more arguments.'

'That's a switch,' she snapped. 'That's supposed to be my line.'

'Gin, you—'

'Don't ''Gin'' me,' she hissed. 'I'm not a child you can growl at when I don't please you.'

'Oh, you please me.' He moved, reaching for her shoulders to drag her into his arms. 'Even when you're grumpy and frustrated you please me.'

She stiffened, loving the feel of him against her but refusing to look up from his tie, knowing he'd see the longing in her face. 'My suggestion is perfectly reasonable,' she croaked. 'And I am not frustrated.'

'You're definitely frustrated.' One finger forced her chin up then he lowered his head, but instead of the kiss she craved he gently bit the curve of her jaw, his other hand caressing her neck. 'But the waiting makes it so much better,' he murmured, his eyes dancing as he registered her parted lips when he lifted his head. 'I promise.'

He grinned at her expression when he released her. 'Stop glaring at me,' he said easily. 'Go home and take a cold shower.'

'I am not frustrated,' she repeated stiffly. 'You exaggerate your charms.'

'If you say so.' The words were conciliatory but there was nothing conciliatory in his widened grin as he ushered her to the door and pushed her firmly into the corridor. 'But if your carotid pulse normally runs along at one-twenty you'd better get Lynn to run off an ECG on you,' he added lightly. He pulled his door shut. 'See you tonight.'

Three hours later Ginny was astounded to find herself parking her car outside the Golden Pavilion. After the embarrassment that had flooded her with Mark's last comment and the knowledge that they both knew her surrender to him was complete, she'd been determined to avoid the dinner, sure that she would soon develop the headache that was going to be her excuse. Oddly it hadn't eventuated.

She'd bathed and dressed mechanically, applied her make-up with shaky hands, and when she couldn't put it off any longer she'd left her flat. Now here she was, exactly where she didn't want to be.

Unfortunately her delaying tactics had only succeeded in making her arrival more conspicuous. 'You're late!' Lynn scolded her with a lopsided smile. She left her seat and came over to greet Ginny as she lingered awkwardly at the entrance to the private room hired for the occasion. 'We've already started to eat.'

She mumbled a apology, dimly registering the richly papered red room, elaborately decorated with golden lanterns, as she let herself be steered towards the huge, circular, white-clothed table that dominated the room.

'The bracelet looks gorgeous,' Lynn whispered. 'Perfect with the necklace.'

'Thanks.' Ginny fingered the gold chain around her neck as she approached the others.

'Of course, Mark's always been good at knowing exactly what you want,' Lynn added quietly, and Ginny shot the nurse a quick, startled look which she met calmly. 'Hungry?'

'A little.' In the centre of the table was a revolving tray, displaying a dozen or so steaming dishes, and their oriental fragrances gently perfumed the room with spicy scents. There were thirty or so people, either eating or milling be-

tween the food table and the bar at the other end of the
room. All familiar faces.

Mark, she saw, was seated, and she refused to acknowledge him, although she'd felt his dark gaze on her from the
minute she'd walked into the room. Instead she concentrated on greeting some of the others at the table.

'Come and let me get you a drink before you sit down,'
Lynn urged, taking her elbow. 'Then eat. You've missed
the soup but the food's wonderful.'

Watching a waiter carrying out a huge silver platter of
prawns, garnished with carrots and cucumbers sculpted into
tiny flowers, she could quite believe it. An hour ago she'd
been sure she wouldn't be able to eat a thing but as she
followed Lynn her stomach grumbled.

A few minutes later she carried her glass back towards
the table. Everybody was seated now, and the conspicu-
ously empty chair that must be hers was opposite Donald
and between Bryan Gould and Mark.

'I won't bite,' Mark said quietly, as she took her place
with a reluctance that must have been obvious.

'You did this afternoon,' she hissed under cover of the
buzz of conversation.

His mouth quirked irritatingly, but before he could say
anything Donald leaned across, interrupting. 'You look particularly beautiful tonight, Virginia.'

Ginny felt Mark stiffen beside her but she managed a
weak smile for the smiling GP, a little uncomfortable as
she remembered the last time he'd complimented her but
relieved he bore no grudges. She appreciated the compli-
ment especially as she suspected she looked more washed-
out than anything else. 'In this old thing?' she joked, ges-
turing to the black sleeveless shift which she really had had
for years.

'Really.' He lifted his glass and toasted her so she had
to take a hurried mouthful of her juice in return. 'You al-

ways look delightful, of course, but tonight you're radiant. You glow.'

She choked, then had to lift an arm to fend off Mark's blows to her back, blows which, she suspected, were more violent than strictly necessary. 'I'm all right,' she protested, glaring at him as she caught her breath. 'I'm all right.' She looked back across at Donald. 'Went down the wrong way,' she explained.

He beamed at her then went back to his food while she sat there, bemused. 'Glowing', he'd said. Well, she knew what that was due to. Weren't pregnant women supposed to glow?

'I should make an announcement before they all start to guess,' murmured Mark.

'Don't you dare.' She sent him a venomous look, trying to assess if he was serious or not, but his return look was bland.

'Rice?' he said calmly, offering her a platter piled with fluffy grains.

Wordlessly she ladled two spoonfuls into the blue and white bowl on the table in front of her then, once he'd replaced the dish on the turntable, she spun it around and helped herself to some of the prawns she'd seen earlier. 'If you say one word I'll kill you,' she said softly, irritated by the flash of his grin before she turned away to talk to Bryan Gould who was seated with his wife on her other side.

'What's happened to your squash career?' Bryan teased. 'Jane says you were good.'

'I was awful,' she said candidly. 'She nearly crippled me.'

They both laughed. 'We should play regularly,' Jane suggested. 'I need more exercise.'

Ginny hesitated. She didn't want to be impolite but, not only did she not want to play, she knew she shouldn't begin vigorous new exercise during her pregnancy. 'I really don't have time at the moment.'

'You have to make time for exercise,' countered Bryan. 'It's an investment in your future.' He leaned forward, catching Mark in a break in his conversation with his neighbour. 'Don't you think Ginny and Jane starting to play squash together is great idea, Mark?'

His brows drew together and the look he shot her was exasperated, but his voice when he spoke was quite calm. 'No, that's not a good idea right now,' he said, speaking loudly enough to make a silence descend over the table. His hand reached for hers and he held it very tightly, as if he thought she might run away. 'You see, we've just discovered we're going to have a baby.'

For one horrible, dreadful moment there was absolute stillness, and then the room erupted with sounds of astonishment and congratulations.

'It had to happen sooner or later,' Mark muttered unrepentantly to Ginny under cover of the noise. 'Shut up and smile.'

Her eyes, already wide with shock, opened further, but there wasn't time to say anything before Donald leaned forward to add his congratulations. 'Good news, you two,' he said stiffly, shaking their hands across the table. 'Keeping the partnership in the family and all that. Ha. Ha.'

Then Lynn rushed over, pressing a kiss to Ginny's icy cheek. 'I knew it, I knew it,' she said, wiping a tear from her eye.

Mark rolled his eyes, apparently in excellent humour. 'That's what you always say, Lynn Carpenter. Admit it. You didn't know a thing.'

Ginny wasn't so sure and Lynn said crisply, 'I'm not as silly as I look, Mark Reynolds.' The nurse was laughing now. 'You think I didn't notice all the carrying on behind closed doors?' She gave Ginny a knowing wink. 'I'm so happy for you both. So you'll be getting married, then?'

'Tuesday morning,' Mark said easily, patting Ginny on the back again when she choked. 'Just a private ceremony. We don't want to wait any longer.' He smiled nastily at her, before giving her a brief, hard kiss on the lips. 'Isn't that right, Gin?'

When he lifted his head she opened her mouth but no words came out. Tuesday? That was only five days away.

Dimly she was aware of accepting everybody's good wishes and numerous toasts, all the while conscious of Mark's hand on hers, his dark eyes watching her every move. To their observers, Ginny realised, he must look adoring, but she knew he was watching for any sign that she'd do something to dispute the impression he was carefully giving that they were both extremely happy.

Once the fuss had quietened and people returned to their meals he released her hand but only after a warning look. 'Eat something,' he muttered under his breath. 'You look about to faint.'

She picked at a few morsels of rice, her face stiff from forced smiling. Five days. 'How did you come up with Tuesday?' she demanded.

'Later,' he growled.

'I thought these things took at least three weeks.'

'Eat.'

For a brief second their eyes clashed but then Ginny broke the contact. In any clash of wills she had little doubt he'd be the victor and it was pointless to pursue it now.

By the time they'd all finished eating it was almost midnight. Mark made a brief speech, thanking everybody for their best wishes, then, after another barrage of congratulations, people began to disperse.

Much as she'd have liked to escape, Mark's firm grip on her arm stopped her leaving his side. 'So, what happens

now?' she asked dully, as he finally walked her towards
her car, the only one apart from his left in the car park.

'I've cut tomorrow morning's clinic back to emergencies
only and organised a locum. I'll pick you up at your flat.
There are several things we need to organise.'

She twirled her keys around her fingers as they stood by
her car, not bothering to suppress her annoyance that he'd
arranged all this without speaking to her first. If things
hadn't gone the way they had tonight, when had he planned
to tell her? Tuesday? 'What sort of things?'

He leaned against the bonnet of her car, studying her
carefully. 'The wedding.'

She straightened. 'Oh, I get to have a say in that, do I?'

'Stop it, Gin.'

'Well, I did rather feel it had been taken out of my
hands,' she said bitterly. 'Don't you think you could have
told me before everyone else?'

He acknowledged her grievance with a lift of the shoulder but his voice was uncompromising. 'You knew I was
organising it and you would have argued whatever I said.'

He was right, but the fact that they both knew that didn't
help. 'Am I allowed to ask what you've arranged?'

'Register office Tuesday at ten-fifteen.' He hesitated. 'I
thought, if you don't mind, my parents could be witnesses.'

She blinked. 'You've told them?'

'This evening.'

'And?'

'And they're very happy. What did you expect? They're
very fond of you.'

'Oh.' Ginny traced a pattern in the gravel with her foot.
'Weren't they surprised?'

His fingers drummed against her car. 'Not particularly,'
he said quietly. 'I imagine they've been expecting it for
years.'

Her head snapped up. 'But surely they realised—'

'We were just good friends?' His mouth twisted. 'I'm not sure they knew what to think.' His look became more penetrating. 'You must realise that everybody assumes we've been lovers, at least in the past if not now. Sarah was convinced.'

She moistened her lower lip. 'W-well, they were all wrong,' she said huskily. 'Sarah was wrong about a lot of things.'

'Mmm.' His eyes dropped to her mouth.

'Did you tell them about the baby?'

He shook his head.

'Why not?'

His mouth compressed. 'They'd think it was the only reason you've agreed to marry me,' he said grittily, his eyes not leaving her mouth which felt as if it was beginning to swell.

She frowned. 'Well, that's true enough.'

'Shut up.' He reached for her, drawing her forward until she stood between his thighs. Very gently and very sweetly, his hand light on the back of her neck, he kissed her until her legs felt as if they would buckle.

When he released her and propelled her away she stared up at him, wide-eyed and bemused. 'Wh-what about my mother?'

'Do you want her to come?'

'I hadn't thought about it,' she admitted shakily. 'Even if there's time, which there might not be, it'd be very expensive and she hates the flight.'

'Of course I'll pay the fares.' He kissed the corner of her mouth. 'But if she really hates flying she might prefer to delay the trip until her grandchild's born.' He frowned. 'Or the three of us could go out there next year. We could get locums for a few months and take a long holiday and introduce the baby to the whole mob at once.'

'I'd like that,' she said shakily. 'Thank you.' For a long

moment their eyes held, and when she let her breath out slowly her thoughts cleared. No wonder she loved him so much, she thought calmly. It was the most natural, real feeling of her life and it stunned her that she hadn't known before because it was so obvious.

'We had fun last time,' he prompted. 'Remember?'

'Yes.' Ginny smiled softly. 'Thanks.'

His eyebrow lifted. 'Problem solved?'

'Yes.' A tiny frown appeared between her brows. 'Mark, you're really sure about this—the marriage?'

'Yes.'

'We could just start by living—'

'No.'

'I'm worried you need to give this more thought.'

'I have.' He tucked her hair behind her ear. 'There's nothing else to discuss.' He took her keys out of her hand and opened the door of her car, waiting until she was seated behind the wheel, her belt fastened, before returning the keys. 'Drive carefully.' He lifted the hand that bore his bracelet and kissed her wrist.

Ginny felt as if she floated home.

The next morning not only did Mark arrive unapologetically late but, instead of greeting her with the sort of kiss he'd given her the night before, he simply nodded curtly and opened the car door.

Ginny tensed, remembering that Sarah was leaving today and that the day before she'd lost the courage to ask him about it. There was a distracted air about him that alarmed her. Was it because he was thinking about Sarah? Was he planning to meet her before she left Norfolk?

With barely a word he drove them directly into town to the register office where they very quickly completed the necessary paperwork and confirmed the date for Tuesday. 'It'll take a while to sort out the sale of your flat,' he said,

as he drove away from the office, 'but we don't have time
to speak with the solicitor before the wedding and I'm away
this weekend.'

Ginny froze. 'What?'

'I promised to help Sarah with her move to Scotland,'
he told her quietly. 'She doesn't have anyone else here to
ask.'

'Oh.' He was turning into her street now and she sat very
stiff in her seat, her gaze fixed on the road outside. 'Of
course. I don't mind.' She didn't know why she felt so
shocked when she had almost been expecting this.

'Ginny...?'

'You don't have to explain anything,' she said quickly.
'It's getting dark over in the west, isn't it? I thought I saw
some lightning earlier. Looks like we're going to have a
storm.'

There was a short, loaded pause, as if he was wondering
whether to make any remark about her comment, but finally
he said, 'There's an agency locum covering your duty tonight. I've arranged for John Newcome to cover Monday
and he'll do all of Tuesday as well. I'll see you Tuesday
morning.'

She swallowed. Tuesday was their wedding day. 'OK.
Fine.'

'Ginny...?' He stopped outside her home and she felt
him turn towards her. 'I'm sorry if you're upset but there's
no reason to be. Please understand. I can't let her down.'

'Of course I'm not upset.' Her voice sounded brittle and
shrill but there wasn't a lot she could do about it. 'Why
would I be upset?' Blindly she fumbled for the doorcatch,
then climbed awkwardly out of the car. 'So, Tuesday, then.'

'I'll pick you up at nine-thirty.'

He sounded very calm but she still couldn't bring herself
to look at him. 'Goodbye.'

She walked away from the car very quickly, tears blurring her vision, dimly aware that he didn't drive off until she was safely inside her flat but that when he did it was fast—as if he was in a hurry to see Sarah.

As soon as she arrived at work she relieved the locum who'd been covering them for the morning. From Lynn's praise it sounded as if he'd done a superb job and the waiting-room was already empty.

Given the week she'd had, she understood why she'd forgotten her promise to call Neil, but when she picked up the telephone that was ringing in the office and recognised his voice Monday's events came back to her in an embarrassed flood and she felt herself flushing hotly as she stammered an apology.

'I wanted to apologise too,' he countered, going on to explain that the reason he hadn't been in touch a lot earlier was that he'd been dating Myra Thomas, the psychiatrist at his hospital, the doctor who had looked after Ginny's patient, Warren Atkins. 'We've actually...' Neil sounded sheepish. 'Well, we've fallen in love,' he said in a rush. 'I suppose Freud would say we—'

'Neil, I don't want to hear about Freud,' Ginny chided, a smile tugging at her lips. 'Or Jung or Pavlov or Skinner or any other of your heroes. You've fallen in love. I know what that's like.' She knew exactly what that was like, she thought, hugging the words to herself. 'Congratulations.'

Neil chuckled. 'Thanks. We've decided to marry. Quite soon, actually. August the first. I'm told it'll take weeks to organise the invitations but I wanted to tell you early so you could pencil us in.'

'That's wonderful. Of course I'll be there.' Genuinely pleased for him, she still couldn't bring herself to tell him her own news—despite the register office visit this morning it didn't seem real yet.

'Please, invite Mark too, of course, to the wedding,' Neil said. 'And Sarah. I drove past them after work this week.

They were walking by the river, but they were kissing and I didn't want to interrupt the romantic moment by stopping.' He continued in a normal voice, naturally unaware of Ginny's pallor, 'Sarah will be settled in Scotland by then but will you pass on the message in case she wants to come down?'

'Of course,' she said stiffly, her chest so tight she could barely talk. Mechanically she managed to get through the rest of the conversation, and after it finished she sagged forward onto her desk.

Obviously Mark wouldn't be spending this weekend just helping Sarah move her furniture. Did he still love her? Had she, Ginny, been all that had come between them? Or was this merely his...final fling?

She realised that while he'd told her he wanted her, and while she'd assumed his honour would ensure it, he'd made no commitment to monogamy. Did he want *both* of them?

She closed her eyes and groaned. She loved Mark but, given that he was marrying her while he was still involved with Sarah, wasn't this marriage simply going to be hell for them all?

Someone from the agency that Mark had used phoned her late that afternoon to explain that the doctor booked to cover her night on call was unwell and wouldn't be able to attend. The staff hadn't been able to organise a replacement at such short notice. Ginny accepted the woman's apology easily, more than willing to cover her own shift, relieved to have something to keep her busy.

She couldn't have hoped for more distractions. The thunderstorm she'd predicted struck late that afternoon and precipitated a flood of asthmatic attacks in the region. It was too inefficient to visit patients one by one so those who sounded bad and lived closer to the hospital than to the practice she advised to go directly to Casualty, while she told the others to come to the surgery to use one of the four nebulisers she'd collected from her own and from the neighbouring practice.

By about midnight the flood had slowed to a trickle and by two her bleeper was quiet. She flung herself into bed, exhausted, and slept dreamlessly until she was called out again at dawn.

It didn't take long to drive to the Jarvis home. 'Thanks for coming, Dr Reid.' The young woman who greeted her when she arrived was a Macmillan nurse but Ginny hadn't met her before. They took a few seconds to introduce themselves to each other and the nurse explained that she'd only begun working in the area two weeks ago. She led Ginny towards the stairs. 'Nellie's just died but I think her daughters would appreciate seeing you.'

Ginny nodded. She'd visited Nellie the last weekend she'd been on call to alter her pain relief slightly. This wasn't unexpected, but she was still saddened and she knew Mark would be.

Sylvia and her sister were sitting by their mother's bed, each holding one of her hands. It was a peaceful little scene. Despite their grief they'd clearly been well prepared.

Sylvia lifted a tear-streaked face. 'She didn't suffer,' she said huskily when she saw Ginny, 'but it's been a long struggle.'

'I know.' Ginny held up her hand when it looked as if the two women were about to stand to leave the room. Usually she felt awkward, making the formal assessment of death with the relatives present, but now, with them so accepting, it felt comfortable. 'No, stay, please, if you want. You're all right there.'

She examined Nellie gently, checking her eyes and listening for heart or breath sounds. She was so tiny and frail. Ginny drew back, blinking quickly.

Muriel stood shakily. 'I'll get you a cup of tea, Doctor.'

'You sit down, Muriel.' Ginny patted the woman's thin

shoulders, exchanging a glance with the nurse who was comforting Sylvia. 'I'll get the tea.'

She slipped out of the flower-filled room, wiping her hands across her eyes. It had been a long twenty-four hours and she was tired and under strain, but she was still aware that the grief she was feeling was deeply genuine. Nellie had been a kind person and a fine mother to her daughters. Now that she'd died something was missing in the world.

The mechanical action of searching through the cupboards for teabags and cups helped, and by the time she carried the tray back up to the bedroom she was feeling calmer.

In these situations in the past she'd always found herself firmly stuck in the role of doctor, either explaining the disease process which had taken the life of a loved one or offering to prescribe sedatives before she made a hasty escape. But now, surprising herself, she discovered she was content to just sit, drink tea and listen to the daughters' random memories, letting the sadness wash over her as well.

'I remember after Dad's funeral,' said Sylvia jerkily, 'she said...that nothing, not even death...could hurt her again...because she knew...she'd be with him then... again.'

'She'll be happy, then,' said Muriel. 'They'll be together.'

Sylvia nodded. 'At last.'

After an hour or so of quiet reminiscing both women looked exhausted. The nurse suggested they tried sleeping and she helped them to their rooms while Ginny filled in the death certificate.

The nurse thanked her again for coming so promptly. 'You've helped them a lot,' she said. 'They're very grateful for all the contact from the practice.'

She nodded. 'My partner knows the family best.'

'Yes. Dr Reynolds was here yesterday morning.'

Ginny lifted her head. She'd assumed he'd gone straight to Sarah's after their appointment at the register office. 'Yesterday?'

'He dropped by before lunch. Just a social call, he said. He did explain about having to go away this weekend and seemed quite upset at the timing, although we both thought Nellie would still be here next week. He spent almost an hour with her, and with Sylvia and Muriel, of course.' She hesitated. 'He's a very...caring person.'

'He is,' she said quietly. How typical of him to want to say goodbye to Nellie properly. 'I'll let him know that she died peacefully.'

She had planned to spend the day tidying her flat and trying to do some work, but by the time she got home she could only just muster enough energy to take a bath. Then, thankful that for once she wasn't suffering any pangs of nausea, she fell into bed.

For the second time that day the telephone woke her. Groggily she rolled over. 'Hello.'

'Ginny? What's wrong?'

'Nothing.' She frowned. 'What time is it?'

'Just before eight. Are you all right?'

She struggled into a sitting position. 'I'm fine, Mark,' she said, her voice tightening as she remembered Sarah. 'Fine. You just woke me up.'

'What are you doing in bed? Are you sick?'

'It's not that late,' she grumbled. 'And it's Saturday. I'm entitled to a sleep-in.'

'For God's sake, it's eight in the evening! What the hell are you playing at?'

She swung her legs out of bed and carried the telephone to the window, sweeping back the heavy curtain to look outside. The sky was still bright but it wasn't morning light, and a couple walked past, giggling and clutching hands, obviously dressed for an evening out. He was right. She'd been asleep over twelve hours. 'I had a busy night on call,' she said vaguely.

'What?' It was more than a shout, it was a roar.

She stiffened. 'The locum couldn't make it,' she said carefully, 'and you're being ridiculous. I'm perfectly capable of working. If you hadn't been such a bully in the first place I'd never have agreed—'

'Quiet, Ginny.' He sounded wearily impatient. 'If you have to sleep the whole of the next day you're obviously less capable than you think.'

This was not the time to explain that it wasn't simply her work but also her anxiety about him which had exhausted her. 'Mark, I'm sorry, but Nellie died this morning.'

He sighed. 'It was coming. It's a release for her but I'm sorry I wasn't there for them. Were the girls all right?'

She smiled. Girls. Both women were in their sixties. 'They're OK,' she said gently. 'They were obviously expecting it. They seemed prepared.'

'As much as you can be,' he said quietly. 'Just a minute, Gin. Sarah's trying to tell me something.' She heard a muffled female voice and Mark saying something indistinguishable in reply, then he was back on the line. 'Sorry about that. Are—?'

She didn't wait for him to continue, needing to know the truth. If he loved Sarah she couldn't go through with this. 'Mark, we've got to talk—'

'When I get back,' he said roughly. 'Gin, I'm worried about you. You should have tried to get another locum and if you couldn't you should have asked Donald to cover the on call. Are you sure you're all right? What about the baby? Are you eating?'

'I'm fine,' she snapped. 'Mark—'

'Tell me what you've eaten today—'

He sounded impatient now but she didn't let him finish. 'Mark, after we get married, were you—are you—planning to be monogamous?'

There was a long pause. Too long. 'What are you expecting me to say to that?' he said carefully.

'I'm not expecting anything,' she said quietly. 'I just want to know.'

There was another pause. A long one. 'Does it make any difference to you what I answer?' he said finally.

A tiny shaft of pain pierced her chest, making her catch her breath. His answer was plain from the way he was avoiding the question.

She heard Sarah's voice saying something again, not clearly enough to hear the words, but Mark spoke quickly before she could give in to the impulse to hang up. 'Ginny, we can't talk about this now. I'll call you when I can.' Abruptly, the line went dead.

# CHAPTER TEN

By MONDAY morning Mark hadn't called, and as his mobile was switched off Ginny had no idea how to reach him. The frustration was driving her mad. Directory enquiries didn't have a new number for Sarah and the switchboard at the main hospital in Aberdeen informed her that they'd never even heard of their new consultant.

It had been, she decided, making desultory preparations for work, one of the worst weekends of her life. She couldn't live with the jealousy, that much was clear. Masochistic images of him entwined with Sarah had haunted her last three nights, but if she couldn't talk with Mark she couldn't tell him the wedding was off.

She ought to look dreadful, she told herself, mystified by her reflection in the bathroom mirror. Despite everything, the glow Donald had mentioned coloured her face. Her complexion looked creamy, instead of washed-out and dull, as she'd expected, and her hair was smooth and glossy. The company that could bottle pregnancy and put it in a skin cream would make a fortune. Then she grimaced, leaning over the toilet as her stomach cramped. That was, as long as they could prevent the side-effects.

Morning surgery was busy but the locum Mark had arranged was competent and familiar with the practice, from covering their holidays in the past, and he insisted she took her half-day as arranged, telling her that Mark had already explained he'd be on his own in the afternoon.

Still Ginny lingered, catching up on paperwork, wanting to make sure that the afternoon wasn't unexpectedly busy before she left. Mark still hadn't called. She felt helpless.

There was no reply at his home and by the number of bleeps on his answering machine she knew he hadn't collected his messages yet.

Mr Heath arrived at the surgery as she was preparing to leave at three. His face was a rosy pink and he'd brought her chocolates. 'To thank you for all your trouble on Thursday,' he explained sheepishly, handing her the box. 'The operation went well and they say she's going to do all right with that eye.'

'I'm very pleased.' Ginny thanked him, assuring him that hard centres were her favourite when he mumbled something about her being able to exchange them if she wanted.

'I'm only sorry I was a bit funny about her going up there to the hospital,' he said gruffly. 'It's been a long time since I've been near one and it's opened my eyes. You were right to be firm. It's a nice place really and the staff are very friendly.'

'I'm glad.' She squeezed his arm, walking with him out to the car park. 'Things have changed a lot in fifty years.'

'For the better,' he agreed, waving as he drove off.

An hour later Ginny grimaced at the frilly outfits on display in the window of a Norwich store, not even understanding why she was there. How many other women, she wondered, had shopped for a wedding dress the day before it was not going to be needed?

When she arrived home she dumped her parcels on the stairs and hurried up to look at her telephone. No messages. Her eyes stung with hot tears of frustration. How dared he do this to her? She pressed the redial button and called his home again but still got only his answerphone.

By eight the next morning she'd been up three hours. She'd dressed, experimentally she'd told herself, changed back into her work clothes, then dressed again. There was still no reply from Mark's home. She even tried his parents' home but there was no answer there so either they were on their way up to Norfolk or they were out early.

Her hands shook so much she ended up looking like a panda on her first attempt at making up her eyes. Miserably she smeared her face with cream, tissued the lot off and started again.

'I hate him,' she muttered. Why was she doing this? There wasn't going to be a wedding. But she couldn't stop herself making the preparations.

By nine she was pacing the floor and by nine-thirty, when she heard his car outside her flat, she was ready to strangle him. 'Where the hell have you been?' she snarled as she met him on the stairs, ignoring the way her nerves clenched at the sight of him, big and powerful in his formal dark suit.

His brows drew together and he glanced briefly at his watch, before looking back at her. 'I'm not late,' he said firmly. 'Ready?'

'No, I'm not ready. I've been waiting for you to call since Saturday!'

'I tried to call a few times but the line was always busy.' Ignoring her outraged gasp he shooed her back up the stairs and towards her room. 'Get whatever you need. We haven't much time.'

'Mark, I'm not going to marry you—'

'Ginny,' he growled. 'It's too late for this. Get your things.'

Her mouth snapped shut. After all the confusion and jealousy and arguing in her head, she was suddenly glad he was making the final decision for her. Like a robot, she collected her hat and bag then let him bundle her out of the flat into warm July sunshine and into his car.

She sat in a silence which he made no attempt to break on the drive into town. With five minutes to spare he parked and when he opened her door she climbed out and preceded him to the building.

His parents were waiting just outside the office. His mother tugged her into a scented embrace. 'We're so happy, Virginia,' she said, pressing a kiss to Ginny's cheek. 'So happy.' She drew back, her look admiring as she studied the calf-length tailored cream sheath Ginny had chosen. 'And you look absolutely gorgeous, as always. So elegant, isn't she, Richard?'

Mark's father nodded and bent forward and lifted her into his own bear-like embrace. 'Welcome to the family, Ginny. About time, hmm?' He exchanged a pointed look with his son. 'After all these years.'

She frowned. Surely they hadn't really thought…?

Mark didn't give her time to collect her thoughts, let alone say anything. 'We haven't much time.' He held open the door to the office and his insistent hand at her back guided her through. 'Think you could manage a smile?' he muttered under his breath as she brushed past him.

She gave him a bemused look. A smile? She was barely managing to stay upright.

The ceremony was performed in a beautifully ornate, quiet room, the air delicately scented by bowls of fresh red roses.

She heard her voice repeat the familiar vows and she was aware of her hand signing the register but it all felt very distant. Even when she emerged into the daylight twenty minutes later and obediently posed for the photographer Mark must have organised, she couldn't quite believe she'd actually gone through with it.

After the photos Mark drove them all to a small country hotel beside one of the Norfolk broads, the large chain of waterways formed centuries before by the flooding of peat-farmed countryside. A white-jacketed waiter opened a bottle of champagne for them in the garden and Mark pushed a flute into her hand when she hesitated. 'I'm not trying to get you drunk,' he said quietly, bending so his mouth grazed her cheek, 'but for their sakes can't you try and play the joyful wife? It's only for a few hours and a couple of glasses won't harm the baby.'

She flushed, burning from the brief contact, and took the glass with a shaky hand.

His father proposed a toast to their happiness and then they strolled around the extensive grounds beside the broad, sipping their drinks. Ginny let the chatter flow gently over her, enjoying the sunshine and the warm pressure of Mark's arm across her back as she listened to the news of his brothers and their families and what had been happening to people they knew in Hampshire.

Afterwards they were served lunch outside on a white, wrought-iron table by the water—a summery meal of cold chicken, salmon and salads, followed by fresh raspberries with thick cream.

She had intended to restrict herself to one glass of champagne but the icy coldness was so pleasant, given the sultry heat of the day, that she let her glass be filled once more without protest. By the time their dishes had been cleared away she was feeling pleasantly relaxed and even a little sleepy, barely mustering the energy to return his parents' kisses when they stood to leave.

'We're getting a cab to Mark's,' his father explained, tapping his trim stomach. 'Too much champagne to face the drive back so we'll spend the night there.'

She started to suggest they all drove back together but Mark didn't let her finish. He steered them away, leaving her alone by the lake. She closed her eyes, listening to the gentle buzz of insects and the soft lapping of the water against the grassy bank.

'Gin...?' His voice was quiet and deep.

Lazily she opened one eye. He was squatting beside her chair, his dark eyes amused. 'Hmm?'

'Wouldn't you be more comfortable lying down?'

She opened her other eye. 'On the grass?'

'No.' He straightened, taking her hand and making her stand up. Without releasing her, he tugged her gently across the lawn towards the hotel, under the entrance arch at the side and then up a tiny, carpeted staircase to one of two low wooden doors on the top floor.

He unlocked the door and pushed it open with his foot, before bending to scoop her into his arms. Seconds later he was laying her on a four-poster bed in the middle of a sunlit room. For a few moments she lay there, wondering.

She heard the sound of the key turning in the door then felt the weight of him kneeling against the bed. Her pulse thudded in her ears and her mouth felt suddenly dry. She couldn't seem to move her eyes from the patterned wooden ceiling. She felt his hands at her ankles. She tensed at the dull thuds which were the sounds of her shoes hitting the floor then gasped as she felt his mouth, warm and determined against the sole of her bare foot.

She levered herself onto her elbows, trying to tug her foot out of his grasp. 'No—'

'Lie down!' He looked up, his eyes so dark they were almost black.

Silently she obeyed, closing her eyes at the exquisite torture of his mouth, again at her feet and then at her ankles below the hem of her dress. He began to inch his way up the fabric, his fingers firm and sure.

When she felt his mouth at her thigh her eyes snapped open. 'Mark—'

'Shh.' His arms slid beneath her hips, bunching her dress at her waist as he dragged her slowly, very slowly, down the bed towards him. At her soft moan of protest he released her, but only to grasp the edges of her underwear.

Gently his hands lifted her, brushing her buttocks with his knuckles as he released them and tugged the briefs away.

She watched him, her breath coming raggedly, as he lowered his head. The picture of him fully clothed while she lay naked from the waist down made her gasp.

For a few moments he rested against her lower stomach, as if listening for their child, and then his hands moved to part her legs. At first she tried to keep them pressed together, but he was powerful and she was aroused. Too aroused to think of anything but this room, this moment.

Hours later she woke surrounded by him. Languidly, her limbs soft and heavy now, she stretched one leg, disentangling it from the hair-roughened pressure of his.

She moved her arm delicately but the movement woke him and with a gentle growl he gathered her back closer into his embrace. 'Keep still.'

Ginny stiffened. His words reminded her of the other demands he'd made before she'd been allowed to sleep, other soft commands whispered against her skin…that she let him touch here…that she moved this way…that she look at him when she…

She groaned. He made her wanton. No wonder Sarah had been so…possessive. The thought invaded her languor like a worm into an apple. Her insides clenched and she curled forward, her fist at her mouth. God! How could she cope with sharing him?

'Gin?' His hand on her stomach drew her back closer into his warmth again. 'What's wrong? Can't you sleep?'

'Let me go,' she said miserably, trying to wriggle free. 'I want to get up.'

He released her, but when she tried to take the sheet to cover herself he sat up, tugging it out of her grip. When she switched on a lamp and grabbed a towel from the chair near the bed he took that, too, flinging it across to the other side of the room. 'Don't hide yourself from me,' he said roughly. 'Not any more.'

'I'm cold.'

His eyes darkened. 'Come back to bed, then. I'll warm you.'

She flushed. 'I'd prefer a bath,' she said tautly. Naked, apart from his bracelet, but refusing to give in to the impulse to shield her body with her hands, she walked stiffly to the bathroom door, locking it pointedly behind her.

No matter how much she wanted to avoid facing him again she couldn't spend for ever in the bath, although she tried. When she eventually emerged her hands and feet were wrinkled and soggy. She wrapped one of the hotel's huge fluffy bath towels around herself sarong-style and straightened her shoulders, before walking out into the bedroom.

He lay on the bed, his hands crossed behind his head. Cool brown eyes registered her towel dispassionately, before rising to her face. 'Clean?'

She nodded and looked away, averting her eyes from where the sheet barely skimmed his hips as she searched for her clothes. 'Yes, thank you.' She hesitated, frowning. 'Where's my dress?'

'I threw it out the window.'

'What?'

He shrugged one broad shoulder. 'You heard me.'

Holding her towel steady, she leaned out of the open window and peered down. Far below, in the faint glow of light from the hotel, she could make out the shape that must be her clothes—and his, too, by the look of it. 'But why?' she demanded hoarsely, backing against the frame as he swung out of bed and headed purposefully towards her.

'Why do you think?' Strong hands pulled away her towel and threw it out the window. While she stood naked and speechless he strode into the bathroom, gathered up the rest of the towels and threw them out as well.

'But—'

'Shut up.' He picked her up and carried her to the bed, dumped her on it then followed her. 'You talk too much,' he said, sliding his hand up to her breast. Before she could protest he covered her mouth with his own.

'No!' She turned her head, kicking out and trying to struggle free, but he was too strong for her.

'Yes,' he said softly, effortlessly holding her still as he bent his head and suckled at the breast his fingers had aroused.

Ginny felt her body arch involuntarily but the realisation that her control was slipping gave her strength. She gripped his hair, forcing him back. 'This is good, isn't it, Mark?'

'It's good,' he muttered.

'Then promise me something,' she said urgently.

He swore, but the grip on her arms lessened and he rolled slightly to one side although her legs remained imprisoned. 'It's too late to make conditions,' he said grimly.

'Just one.'

His eyes narrowed. 'Go on.'

She swallowed. 'I want you to stop seeing Sarah,' she said tightly, freeing her legs and rolling to face away from him, pulling the sheet so it covered her. 'Give us a chance first.'

He said nothing. All she could hear was the pounding of her own heart. 'I realise you weren't expecting me to ask this,' she continued after a few awful minutes, 'but for the sake of our child—'

'What the hell are you talking about?' he demanded forcefully.

She rolled back. He was looking at her as if she were mad. 'I know you still love her,' she said huskily.

His brows drew together. 'Don't be ridiculous.'

'I want you to stop seeing her,' she said, enunciating each word clearly.

'Sarah's in Scotland.'

'I know that.' She glared at him. 'There are such things as flights and cars and telephones, you know.'

He shook his head briefly as if to clear it. 'I helped her with moving, but that's all, Ginny. You think I'm still involved with her?'

'Neil saw you together,' she said stiffly. 'Walking by the river. Last week.'

'Yes?'

She drew an unsteady breath. 'You were kissing,' she said, her voice so faint it was barely audible. 'I realise you're still in love with her,' she whispered, 'but we're married now.'

His soft curse made her start. 'Ginny, you're mad. Why the hell do you think I've married you? Why do you think I've forced you to go through with this?'

'For the baby.' She hauled herself out the other side of the bed, taking the sheet as well and holding it in front of her. 'And perhaps the…sex.'

She saw his jaw tighten and backed, but he was too fast for her. He hurtled from the bed, ripped her sheet away, walked to the window and threw the sheet out to join the other things on the ground below. 'I won't let you hide from me,' he said grimly. 'Yes, I want the baby and I want the sex, but that's not all. Yes, Sarah and I met last week to discuss…things. We went for a walk and I probably kissed her goodbye, but I haven't shared her bed for months—' He broke off. 'For God's sake, Ginny! What sort of man do you think I am?'

She crossed her hands across her breasts. 'You stayed with her,' she cried. 'You were with her when you called me on Saturday night.'

'I didn't try to hide that from you. I stayed with her but

I didn't sleep with her, you idiot.' He crossed back to her and tugged her arms apart, watching the way her breasts instantly hardened. 'You have a beautiful body. Let me look.'

'No!' she sobbed, hating herself for the way her body betrayed her.

'Ginny, stop it. There's no need for this.' He took her gently into his arms and lifted her back onto the bed so she lay on top of him, her face against his chest. 'I want you so much I couldn't look at another woman if I tried,' he said softly. 'Last weekend was just about helping a friend.'

'It wasn't just a weekend—it was four days!'

'I think I like you being jealous.' He nuzzled her head. 'I only stayed Saturday. I spent Sunday night and yesterday in Hampshire, helping Dad and his partner. I promised weeks ago to help them install their practice's new computer system. Neither of them had a clue where to start.'

'When we spoke on Saturday you told me you didn't want to be monogamous.'

'No, I didn't.' His teeth at her ear lobe made her shiver. 'I said we couldn't talk about it then.' He shifted to her other ear. 'But now I've got you exactly where I want you we can talk about it. I'm not letting you play around, Ginny, and I'll never let you leave.'

She lifted her head, her face dazed. 'Ever?'

'Ever.' He slid lower to lick at her aching breasts. 'You're my wife and you can't run away any more.' He made a soft sound against her skin. 'God, I love you!'

'You love me?' She was faint.

He lifted his head. 'Passionately.'

'I'll never want to run away,' she whispered. 'Mark, I love you too.' She meet his dark gaze with shy courage. 'Why didn't you tell me?'

'Shh.' He shifted to her mouth again, urgent now. 'Later,' he murmured. 'Let me love you.'

'I have a terrible confession,' she whispered later, much later, when they lay entwined and still. 'That night, when I came to your house, I suspect my motives might have been less…pure than I pretended.'

His chuckle was warm against her stomach. 'You mean you intended to seduce me?'

'It's not funny.' She tugged gently at his hair. 'When it looked like you were getting serious about Sarah I felt a bit…unsettled. I didn't want to lose you. And I'd been thinking a lot about babies and things. Subconsciously I might have deliberately set out to—'

'Seduce me,' he said conversationally, kissing a tiny freckle on her hip.

'You think this is a joke,' she cried, twisting to escape his teasing caress. 'Listen to me. I'm serious.'

'You can't do something subconsciously and deliberately,' he told her lightly. 'And even so I wouldn't have objected. I'd wanted you for years.'

She swivelled, wide-eyed. 'What?'

Mark laughed at her astonishment. 'Ginny, be reasonable. Of course I did.'

'I never guessed.'

'You weren't supposed to.' His hand curved over her breast and he stroked her, softly, absently. 'I'm a man and it was a physical thing. You never gave me any hint that you might respond and our friendship was too important to me to risk upsetting it so nothing happened. But then Neil came along.'

She blinked. 'Neil?'

'He was the first man you'd ever dated for more than a couple of months,' he explained. 'It didn't take long for me to start feeling possessive.'

He cupped her, then bent and kissed the breast his hand enclosed, sending a little tremor of delight across her skin. 'I suspect that half the reason I let things continue with

Sarah was that the way I felt about you and Neil was worrying me. When she asked me to come to Glasgow the choice was never between Sarah or Norfolk—it was Sarah or you. Almost as soon as I told you I was considering leaving things began falling into place and I realised I couldn't go.

'That night you came to dinner, you and Neil—before you arrived I told her I wasn't going with her to Scotland. That was the reason she was so upset, so angry with you. I knew it wasn't the best time to break it to her—I'd only just decided—but she'd made too many plans and things were getting out of hand.'

Ginny swallowed, remembering how disturbed Sarah had seemed. So they hadn't been making love after all. 'She called you "sweetheart",' she said hollowly.

He shrugged. 'For your benefit, probably. She never believed you didn't have anything to do with my decision.'

'And she—'

'Was disappointed,' he told her. 'And angry, deservedly angry for a while, although it was me who deserved it, not you. I hadn't realised how serious she was.' His thumb toyed with her already erect nipple. 'It was never the way it is between us,' he said huskily.

She watched his hand against her flesh, lifted herself closer to him. 'You never explained anything.'

'I assumed my feelings were transparent. Remember, I was jealous of anyone who came near you—Donald, Neil, even that student. You must have known there was something odd about that.'

'I was jealous too.' Her other breast longed for his touch and she guided his hand across, closing her eyes weakly at the pleasure of his caress. 'All weekend when you were with Sarah…'

'I'm glad.' Mark kissed her, a brief, hard, passionate kiss. 'I know it hurts but I'm glad you felt that, too.'

'I couldn't go through that again.'

'You won't ever have to,' he said flatly, tucking her hair behind her ears. 'Neither of us will.' He smiled ruefully. 'Now my ring's on your finger I think I might just be able to control my blood pressure when you mention another man's name in my hearing.'

'I love you.' Propping herself up on one elbow, she drew a tiny heart on his chest. 'Perhaps I've always loved you. Perhaps that's why I could never find anyone else.' She drew another heart against his stomach. 'If it hadn't been for the baby, what would have happened?'

He captured her sliding finger with a growl. 'The baby was a wonderful surprise but I would have seduced you again. I was giving you a few months to calm down and then—wham!' His hands slid to the gap between her thighs and he laughed at her startled squeak. 'I already knew I could...excite you. The rest I was prepared to work on.'

She raised her head, affronted by his confidence. 'For your information,' she said stiffly, 'it wouldn't have been that easy.'

'For your information,' he teased, 'I planned to tie you to my bed, ravish you until you were too exhausted to fight and then force you to marry me.'

'Oh.' She pouted. 'Does that mean I don't get to be tied up and ravished now?'

Mark laughed. 'I think we can come to some arrangement,' he said, sliding down her body to kiss her stomach, 'but I've thrown the rest of the sheets out the window. If it's binding and ravishing you want you'll have to run down and get them.' He nuzzled her thighs. 'Naked.'

Ginny sat up. 'I suppose it is dark.'

He grinned. 'Not that dark.'

'And I suppose there aren't many people around.'

'Only an entire hotel's worth,' he countered.

She frowned at him. 'It's not as if people haven't seen a naked woman before.'

'Perhaps not outside their room.'

'Running downstairs would be good exercise.'

'I can think of better.' His hands slid her thighs apart. 'Let me see you.'

'Mark?'

'Hmm?'

'I'm very shy really.'

He lifted his head, grinning. 'I'll get them,' he said softly. 'Witch.' He eased himself away from her then bent to kiss the skin her hand had modestly covered. 'Wait for me, Gin.'

'I'd wait for you for ever.'

Their son was born on 18 January, a seven-and-a-half-pound dark-haired baby with Mark's chin and Ginny's eyes. They named him Richard James after his grandfather and loved him dearly.

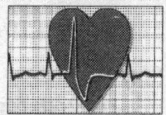

## MILLS & BOON®

# Next Month's Romance Titles

♡

Each month you can choose from a wide variety of romance novels from Mills & Boon®. Below are the new titles to look out for next month from the Presents™ and Enchanted™ series.

## *Presents*™

| | |
|---|---|
| THE SPANISH GROOM | Lynne Graham |
| HER GUILTY SECRET | Anne Mather |
| THE PATERNITY AFFAIR | Robyn Donald |
| MARRIAGE ON THE EDGE | Sandra Marton |
| THE UNEXPECTED BABY | Diana Hamilton |
| VIRGIN MISTRESS | Kay Thorpe |
| MAKESHIFT MARRIAGE | Daphne Clair |
| SATURDAY'S BRIDE | Kate Walker |

## *Enchanted*™

| | |
|---|---|
| AN INNOCENT BRIDE | Betty Neels |
| NELL'S COWBOY | Debbie Macomber |
| DADDY AND DAUGHTERS | Barbara McMahon |
| MARRYING WILLIAM | Trisha David |
| HIS GIRL MONDAY TO FRIDAY | Linda Miles |
| BRIDE INCLUDED | Janelle Denison |
| OUTBACK WIFE AND MOTHER | Barbara Hannay |
| HAVE BABY, WILL MARRY | Christie Ridgway |

On sale from 7th May 1999

H1 9904

*Available at most branches of WH Smith, Tesco, Asda, Martins, Borders, Easons, Volume One/James Thin and most good paperback bookshops*

# 2 FREE

## books and a surprise gift!

We would like to take this opportunity to thank you for reading this Mills & Boon® book by offering you the chance to take TWO more specially selected titles from the Medical Romance™ series absolutely FREE! We're also making this offer to introduce you to the benefits of the Reader Service™—

- ★ FREE home delivery
- ★ FREE gifts and competitions
- ★ FREE monthly Newsletter
- ★ Exclusive Reader Service discounts
- ★ Books available before they're in the shops

Accepting these FREE books and gift places you under no obligation to buy, you may cancel at any time, even after receiving your free shipment. Simply complete your details below and return the entire page to the address below. *You don't even need a stamp!*

**YES!** Please send me 2 free Medical Romance books and a surprise gift. I understand that unless you hear from me, I will receive 4 superb new titles every month for just £2.40 each, postage and packing free. I am under no obligation to purchase any books and may cancel my subscription at any time. The free books and gift will be mine to keep in any case.

M9EA

Ms/Mrs/Miss/Mr ..............................Initials.................................
BLOCK CAPITALS PLEASE

Surname ...............................................................................................

Address ...............................................................................................

..............................................................................................................

......................................................Postcode ...................................

**Send this whole page to:**
**THE READER SERVICE, FREEPOST CN81, CROYDON, CR9 3WZ**
**(Eire readers please send coupon to: P.O. BOX 4546, DUBLIN 24.)**

Offer valid in UK and Eire only and not available to current Reader Service subscribers to this series. We reserve the right to refuse an application and applicants must be aged 18 years or over. Only one application per household. Terms and prices subject to change without notice. Offer expires 31st October 1999. As a result of this application, you may receive further offers from Harlequin Mills & Boon and other carefully selected companies. If you would prefer not to share in this opportunity please write to The Data Manager at the address above.

Mills & Boon is a registered trademark owned by Harlequin Mills & Boon Limited.
Medical Romance is being used as a trademark.

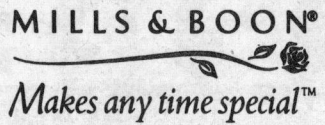

# MILLS & BOON®

*Makes any time special*™

# The Regency Collection

**Mills & Boon® is delighted to bring back, for a limited period, 12 of our favourite Regency Romances for you to enjoy.**

**These special books will be available for you to collect each month from May, and with two full-length Historical Romance™ novels in each volume they are great value at only £4.99.**

**Volume One available from 7th May**